A Bouquet of Love Stories

Anjana L

With Best regards
to Raj

d. Anjana
9880923526

notionpress
.com

INDIA · SINGAPORE · MALAYSIA

Notion Press

No.8, 3rd Cross Street
CIT Colony, Mylapore
Chennai, Tamil Nadu – 600004

First Published by Notion Press 2020
Copyright © Anjana L 2020
All Rights Reserved.

ISBN 978-1-64983-952-7

Dedication

I dedicate this book to my dear family
for their love and support. My mother Srilakshmi,
my sister Anupama and her husband Venkatesh
Prasad and their son Ankith. My dear brother Anirudha,
who was the reason for
my writing and his wife Shruti. I thank my cousin,
Eshwar and his wife Srividya and their daughter Isha for
their support as well. My dear friends Jyothi
and Hemalatha and Hema, thank you. And last
but not the least, my big brother,
Aniruddha, for his support.

Contents

Almost Sati

Sia was awakened by the groans of her husband, Ramesh on the hospital bed. She quickly pressed the nurse call button and in no time a nurse appeared by the bedside. The nurse checked his BP, pulse rate and heart rate on the monitors attached to the bed and rushed to call the doctor.

When the doctor came, he called Sia aside and informed her that it was time to let go and therefore she should inform their relatives. It was a matter of time before Ramesh passed on. There was nothing much they could do now. They kept vigil throughout the night and in the morning, at 8 AM, Ramesh left his body. Sia hoped for his heavenly abode but she knew there was little chance of that happening. She did not shed a single tear. She felt the burden that was her marriage lifting from her shoulders and felt light-headed.

She quickly got out of the melancholic atmosphere and called Ramesh's parents to inform them which in turn led to his mother venting her ire at her. According to Sia's mother in law, she was the root of all the mishaps that ever visited her son. How much ever Sia tried to detach herself from the venom that her mother-in-law spewed, there was a corner in her heart that got hurt by the sheer injustice of it all. She took a deep breath and called her father, Satish

Sharma. Her father said, "Good riddance to bad rubbish," and said he would come to the hospital as soon as possible to attend to the next steps. Sia and her parents knew that Ramesh's parents would not lift a finger to help monetarily, physically or emotionally.

It was a relief to Sia that her parents also stayed in Bangalore as herself and were a big support to her. There was a slew of relatives all over Bangalore as well, among which, some were cordial and some were not. It was enough for her that her family was with her through thick and thin. Her family consisted of her father, Satish Sharma, mother, Shanta Sharma, and her younger brother, Sharath Sharma. As she was musing about her family, they arrived and Satish immediately took charge of the situation and made arrangements for the funeral. Ramesh's parents refused to come for it. His mother was screaming in the background that Sia had come into their lives and taken their son's life. Satish quickly disconnected and handled the cremation.

Sia and her family then proceeded to Sia's house, where she packed her belongings and went to stay with her parents. She needed the comfort that her parents provided to renew her goals in her work life. She was a freelancer in the world of interior designing, having done a diploma in it after her degree in psychology. She had a team that worked with her based on the clients she got. Her work life was suspended for the past 6 months as Ramesh had to be hospitalised, as he was diagnosed with 3rd stage pancreatic cancer. She was married to him for 6 months.

She got married to Ramesh, a thug because she was blackmailed. He had evidence, albeit forged, which could have sent her father to jail until he was deemed not guilty by the court. Also, he and his parents had threatened that they would kill her family if she declined to marry him.

After marriage, she got to know that he had cancer and was in pain most of the time. His parents for the most part stayed in Chennai but kept the grapevine going with calls 2 to 3 times every day. The plan was to impregnate her so that Ramesh had a son and his name would live on. Sia did not allow him to touch her and he could not force her as he was a weakling physically. She kept her ears and eyes open and zeroed in on the evidence and destroyed it.

She had kept the reason to herself. Her family was deeply hurt when she took this decision. She was a smart entrepreneur at 27 and they had bright prospects for her and could not fathom this decision of hers. But they kept the faith and she figured this was the time to tell them.

Satish was flabbergasted by this piece of information and he was furious with me. He told me his record at work and as a citizen was clean and they couldn't have made it stick. He made me promise I would tell him things like this in future.

I then decided to put the past 6 months in the back burner in my head and focus on my work. I renewed old contacts and my team and tried to get work based on my previous work history. I called my previous clients and informed them that I was rebuilding my career.

Some were work friends and asked about the reason for my 6-month break. I just said it was a family emergency. I had a small office on the terrace of my parents' house which I loved. It had an entrance from the road and I loved it. I went to the terrace to reclaim it. It was clean and not one article was out of its original place. I thanked my mom and went in and sat in my office.

Soon everyone in my area of work got to know that I was back in business and I started getting work. I got into work with renewed vigour and kept the past strictly in the past. So much so, that the past 6 months which was so difficult to me, seemed a mere nightmare after 3 months. But it seemed I spoke too soon.

Suddenly Ramesh's parents descended on us and asked me to pack my bags and go to Chennai with them. I figured to be their unpaid maid. My dad filed a police complaint against them for intimidation, blackmail and threatening to kill. They were arrested and convicted in the court of law. This became news for fodder in our community and the grapevine was abuzz with it. This did not impact my work adversely. And since I had no intention of getting remarried, it did not affect my personal life as well. At least that was what I thought.

One fine Saturday, about 4 months after Ramesh's death, my mother asked me to get ready for a pre-wedding

function at my cousin's place. It was a ladies-only function. I put on a nice new salwar kameez and minimum makeup and jewellery, a small bindi on my forehead and went with my mother to the designated place.

I got the feeling that I was a celebrity since all the conversations stopped on our arrival and I was appraised from head to toe and disapproval emanated from those who were present there.

"Do you know you cannot go out for 1 year after your husband's death," my aunt asked. Both my mother and I just looked at her and turned around and exited the place and my mother was still in shock when we reached home. My dad called my uncle, at whose house the function was held, and told him that obviously, we were not part of their family and that we would not attend the functions any more.

As I sat there with my family, I suddenly realised that I was not invited to the Gruhapravesh of any client that I had worked for in the 4 months after Ramesh's death. I voiced this to my family and my father drily said, "So apparently we are still living in the dark ages." Sharath switched on the Gaana app and turned on some retro songs and we absorbed it and could feel the tension lifting from our inner selves. Our family was addicted to old Hindi songs. Sharath danced with my mother and my father said, "Can I have this dance?" to me and I sprung up and we all danced our weariness away.

2 men, who appeared to be in their mid 30s, entered my office the next day. They introduced themselves as Siddharth and Abhimanyu. Both were handsome. They wanted to consult me about interior designing for Siddharth's new villa. He took over the conversation and described his property. The villa had 4 bedrooms and a basement and he wanted the décor to be warm and different and most importantly comfortable as his parents would be living with him. It was located in outskirts of Bangalore.

I showed them some of my work which I catalogued after the interiors were completed with the owner's permission. I also gave them references to my old clients, so that they could check for themselves. Siddharth asked if I was in the middle of some commission /work that would keep me busy. I said I was in the completion stage of 2 assignments and would be free in 2 week's time. He said the timelines worked for him and we shook hands. I handed them my visiting card and my quote for the assignment and they left.

I then closed my office and went down to my parents' house. My dad was back from his workplace. He was a mechanical engineer in a factory which was one of the top industries in India. I offered to make tea for everyone. This was the best place and the company that I loved most. We sat and did some chit chat and I told them about my visitors. My dad was very happy with the news. New assignments were always good. He told me, "This means your name is among one of the best talents in this business." I grinned at him and agreed.

I got a message on my Whatsapp after a week and a half from Siddharth and he asked for a good time to call. I responded by saying after 30 minutes as I was in a client's place and handing over everything after the completion of work. I got a call from him as I was walking back to my car after exactly in 30 minutes. I was mildly impressed. This was rare, I thought to myself and took the call. He asked if I was free for his assignment and I agreed. The 2nd assignment was completed before the due date and I was free to take on the new job.

He said he would like to meet in his villa and have a discussion on exactly what he wanted. I said I could meet the next day and then work on the designs. We fixed a time for the meeting and he said he would pick me up from my house. I protested and said I could drive myself to the site if he sent me the location on Google Maps. He disagreed and said he would be at my place by 11 AM and disconnected.

I wondered how a man who was a strategy officer in a big multinational company could have so much time. It helped my cause, but I would miss the mobility which I strongly held on to for the longest time, which was the reason I got a car as soon as I could.

He was on time the next day and came in an SUV. I introduced him to my mother and he did a namaste and we got going. I was dressed in green trousers and a light green top. He looked at me appreciatively and I seconded the look. He was in blue jeans and a white shirt. He said the drive to his villa from my place was about 45 minutes and he sent me the Google Map then. I thought we could catch up on the dimensions and his ideas about the assignment, but he switched on music and it was just the kind I liked. Old English songs.

By the time we arrived at our destination, we were both in a good mood and ready for work. The villa was empty and he took me around it. It was a 4 bedroom house with one hall on the ground floor and one bedroom and 3 rooms on the 1st floor and a basement. There was place on the ground floor for a foyer and car park and a small garden. There was a pantry on the 1st floor and a portion for a portico which could be used as a garden or terrace or both.

All in all, it was a beautiful house and I got some ideas as I looked at the house. We sat in the kitchen where there were 2 stools and a small table. We sat there for the discussions. I took out my work pad and a pencil and asked him to give me the conditions and ideas he had. He smiled and kept the pad aside and said he would make some coffee.

It was instant coffee and it was well made. I drank it and waited for him to start the meeting. He finished and said, "Carte blanche. Assume this is your house and design it the way you would want it." I tried again, "But you will have some ideas about how you want it designed?" He shook his head. I then asked if his parents were particular about some things. He said their room was on the ground floor and they liked traditions. That's it.

The freedom his words gave was tremendous, It meant I didn't have to work around the client's vision. My vision was working overtime. I gave him the contract I normally give my clients and he read it and signed it with a flourish. I gave him a copy and expected to get a cab and go to my office to draw up the plans. He had other plans.

He said, "Can you show me the ideas if you already have any."

Clearly, he had plenty of time today, I thought to myself. He grinned at the expression on my face. "I have taken the day off and I work from home mostly."

"Then you should have a study?" I asked him.

He said the place next to the stairs on the 1st floor could work as a study. He said anyway the whole of the 1st floor was his and he could work anywhere. I made a mental note about this and sat to draw up the plans. He sat on the stairs and opened his laptop. There was a friendly camaraderie in the atmosphere. He switched on Old Hindi songs on his laptop and the atmosphere changed for the better.

I smiled and he caught that. I had 2 plans in about 2 hours for the whole house and we sat down to discuss it. He approved the 1st one in its broad structure. I told him I would send the details in 2 days. He said, "Take your time. The end of the week is good enough."

I gave him a surprised look. "What are your timelines? "I asked him and he said, "6 months."

I thought that was luxurious. I said, "I appreciate the time."

It was almost 3 PM by then. So I asked him if I could book a cab and be on my way. He blankly refused and said he would drop me after a delayed lunch at a restaurant. I realised that he just takes over without asking me about my interests. But I admitted to myself that it felt good. So I agreed. This was not new. I made friends with my clients and we had lunch or coffee outside many times.

We went to his parked SUV and he opened my door and waited till I had settled in completely with the seat belt. Then he went to the driver's side and hopped in. He said there was a nice restaurant which was pure veg and asked me if it suited me. I wondered briefly if he could read minds as well. I said since I was a vegetarian, it suited me. He said, "Ditto."

It was a 10-minute drive and we got nice seats overlooking the small garden and the pool. He let me choose and I chose Chana Batura for us and sat sipping the mocktail which arrived early. He looked at me and said, "So, do you have a boyfriend?"

I gaped at him aghast. He wanted to talk about our personal lives and not work. With a sigh. I said, "No, I am a widow."

He looked shocked for a short while before he got his emotions under control. "What happened?" was his next question. No 'sorry' or 'condolences'. I noted that and decided to be as matter of fact as he was being. I said, "Cancer. I was married for 6 months."

I hoped he would drop the topic when the food arrived. He barely looked at it. "Did you not know that he had cancer? Why did you marry him?"

I was royally irritated by then. I told him that I was blackmailed. Ramesh was a thug and my dad got his kin arrested after his death. After his death, because I had kept the reason for my marriage a secret from him. Siddharth looked at me after he got every bit of information from me and said, "Women. I wish I met you before his death. I would have enjoyed talking to him."

I closed my eyes and said I was fed up of this topic and he decided to say he was sorry. Bad memories. I wanted to irk him, so I asked him about his love life. He grinned and said, "1 failed relationship," and he was glad it was over. He said she turned out to be a bitch and he was relieved to be rid of her. "Let's eat," he said and his good humour seemed to have returned. He asked me if my father would be at home as he wanted to talk to him about my deceased husband. I said yes. He said, "Good, let's proceed."

With a flourish, he said, "After you," and we walked back to the SUV.

He started the vehicle and sensed my mood and with a half-smile, he switched on music and I calmed down a bit by the time we reached my house. He let me lead the way inside my house for which I was grateful and I told him so. He laughed and said, "Once in a while."

My parents were in the drawing-room sipping tea and they stood up when I marched in with Siddharth walking behind me. I introduced him to my parents in a cross tone. Satish and Shanta looked at each other and smiled. Siddharth plonked himself on the empty chair and looked at me expectantly. "What?" I asked him. He shook his head vigorously and said, "Sit."

I sat and glared at him. "He wanted to talk to you about Ramesh," I said to my dad and we all looked at him. He told me, "Don't you have to change and lock your office or something?" I looked at my dad and he said, "Yes, my child, why don't you go and do both?' I stomped up the staircase and I could hear their laughter following me.

I did both the tasks that were assigned to me by his Highness and came down a good half hour later. They were sipping on tea again and my mom stood up to make some for me. I had cooled down by then, so I said I would get it and went into the kitchen and made some tea for myself. "You didn't tell me you can cook," his highness said, drawing smiles from my parents. I said, "Making tea is not cooking and you didn't ask and I didn't know that it was a criteria for designing a villa."

He grinned at me and said it wasn't. He looked at my parents and said he had to leave as he had a meeting to attend online. Thankfully, he didn't ask if he could use my office nor did my parents offer. They shook hands and he winked at me and left.

I sat fuming. My parents just put on some music and sat listening to it. I cooled down again and said I had work to do for his Highness and went to my room.

I was fully focussed on my work for 3 days and came up with a detailed plan for Siddharth's house. I sent the hard copy of the plan to his address and a soft copy to his email id that he had furnished for this purpose. Then I waited for his response. My mail checker said he had received it. Since I didn't have any other assignments at that moment, I sat in my house in front of the TV and thought I would catch up on some movies my brother had recommended. Just then, I saw his SUV from the window.

I went outside just as he was parking his vehicle. I asked him if he wanted to discuss anything regarding the detailed plan I had sent. "No," he said. "I came to have tea with your mother. Your father is on his way home. So we can all catch up."

By now, you would think I would be used to his strange behaviour. But I wasn't. "What about my plan?" I persisted. By now we were in the drawing-room.

"I approved them through mail," he said. My mother wished him and went into the kitchen to make tea and some snacks that she was halfway through.

My dad appeared right on time and he hugged me and said, "Do you mind going up to your room, my dear? I will tell you everything tonight, I promise." I smiled at him and went to my room and started doodling. I heard Siddharth's SUV starting and he left after about an hour. My dad appeared in my room along with my mom and they were in a sombre mood. So I just sat and waited for the news from Ramesh's kin.

My dad took a deep breath and said, "Siddharth and I have been doing some investigation with the help of private detectives and we have proof that 2 people who are Ramesh's kin are planning something against you. They are also trying for bail for his parents. The police has advised protection for our family. Siddharth is helping by getting the best bodyguards for us and for you especially. He will come every day to pick you up and the bodyguards will accompany him along with you."

I nodded to appease my dad and mom. I would tell Siddharth that I could go in my car with the bodyguards. I realised that he may not agree so easily. But I thought it was worth a try. I hugged my mom and dad and told them not to worry. They left with a smile and a tear.

The next day, promptly at 9 AM, both Siddharth and our bodyguards arrived. My brother thought they were cool. I wanted to ask him if that was for Siddharth. He left for work. He was a BE graduate and had recently bagged a good job at a good company. Siddharth shook hands with him and Sharath looked happy. He went on to tell my brother about the precautions he would have to take and Sharath listened with rapt attention. He then left after blowing kisses at all of us.

Siddharth then asked me if I was ready and I was. I had worn a pale pink salwar suit and my hair in a ponytail. "Don't you ever let your hair loose?" he asked. My dad answered for me, "At the workplace, this will be easy to manage."

They both looked at me and smiled at each other. Friends, I thought. I left with him after hugging my parents. "They will be fine," Siddharth said when we had settled in his car. "These bodyguards are the best at what they do."

"Siddharth, thank you," I said and he looked at me and said, "My friends call me Sid."

I said, "Oh, but I like Siddharth."

"Likewise," he said amidst the laughter from my bodyguard and his highness.

"What is short for Sia?" he asked.

"That's easy," I said. "It's Si." Another round of laughter from the 2 men. He tweaked my hair and said, "Angel is short for Sia."

I was startled but pleased. I kept quiet. My bodyguard, Shankar who was sitting at the back said, "I agree."

Siddharth looked at him and raised his eyebrows and Shankar fell quiet.

We reached his house in contemplative silence and I saw that my team was already present there. The material that I had indented had also arrived. I introduced Siddharth and Shankar to them and we got down to work. Siddharth again went and sat on the stairs and switched on his laptop and played that beautiful song playlist of his. I was on the move, getting the materials in the right room and drawing-room. Suddenly coffee appeared and Siddharth had arranged for some snacks and our tiny hunger pangs were silenced. He said lunch and evening tea and snacks would be made available. I was impressed. So were my team. I thanked him and said this was unexpected. He said it was his assignment and his rules. We all agreed in unison and got back to work.

This was our routine for the week that followed. Early next week, my brother saw some people loitering near our house and my dad and Siddharth and our bodyguards rounded them up and took them to the police station for interrogation. There was an attempt to get bail for Ramesh's parents once again, but it was shot down by the judge.

After the interrogation, we got to know that there was a plan to kidnap me and ask for a ransom and then do away with me. My dad hugged Siddharth for his timely help and his strategy. Satish told me he was a well-wisher of our family. I agreed. The criminals were jailed and the case would be on fast track according to Siddharth. He wanted to be in the courtroom with my dad and my dad readily agreed.

My mom wanted all of us to attend and my dad agreed to it. The last time my dad had disagreed and took my brother alone. He was more relaxed this time around and I attributed it to Siddharth. I looked at him and said, "Thank you." He put his arm around me and side hugged me. "I am here always, remember that," he said.

My mom suggested dinner out and everyone readily agreed. We said we would meet Siddharth at the restaurant. He disagreed. "We will go in my car. Everyone will fit in nicely." He said he kept a spare shirt in his car. My dad showed him the guest room.

The restaurant had organised a ghazal concert and we enjoyed it as well as the food. Siddharth and my family got along like a house on fire. When the bill came, my dad picked it up and told Siddharth, "Next time." He agreed smiling. We reached home by 10 PM and he left for his rented accommodation soon after.

The court date came and it was for the next week. We all packed into his SUV and left for the court on the designated date. We sat at the back in the courtroom as per my dad's wishes. It was over in 1 and a half hours. No new dates. They were convicted and sent to jail for the same crime as Ramesh's parents and that was the end of it.

My family and Siddharth looked at me keenly, for the hour and a half, there were attempts to malign my name and character. The sitting judge sustained the objections of our lawyer. But they called me a slut and a bitch of a woman who did not care about her husband. I internalised the shock of it and smiled at them a trifle sadly and said I was fine. I looked at my dad and said, "I have lived with them for 6 months. You would think I was accustomed to this talk by now." He hugged me and led me back to the car.

Sharath looked at Siddharth and said, "Do you think this is the end of it?" Siddharth said it appeared so, but they would have a discussion with the police and then call off the bodyguards. He asked Sharath, "What will make your sister happy other than old music?"

I said, "Nature."

He said, "I know just the place."

My parents and Sharath begged off and said they had work to do. My mom said, "Go with him, child. We will get a cab."

Siddharth took me to Lal Bagh and we sat there for an hour enjoying nature. He asked me about my life with Ramesh for 6 months and I told him it was mostly asking me to do all work and cursing me a lot and trying to impregnate me.

"He was confined to his bed most of the time and in pain. I just handed him the tablets at the right time and took him to the doctor when it was scheduled. It was hell," I told him. "I deliberately kept my communication with my family to the minimum but they didn't give up. They were with me throughout. My parents visited every day and Sharath on weekends."

After that, I fell silent and he let the silence envelop us and put his arm around my shoulder. I took a deep breath after an hour and said I was okay. He stood up, pulled me up and we walked back to the car. The ride back was good, in silence. He walked with me to the house and then bid goodbye to my family and then left.

The next day I thought I would drive myself to the workplace, in this case, his house. But I was mistaken. Promptly at 9, he came to pick me up and Shankar also came.

I asked my dad and he said that just to be on the safe side, we were retaining the bodyguards till the month-end. By then the police would have connected all the dots. It was Siddharth's idea. I agreed with his thought process and left with him to work.

It was 1 and a half months since I took up the assignment and the house was looking beautiful. My first step was his study, but he still sat on the staircase. I asked him why. And he said he was scared to sit alone in the study. "Right," I said and left it at that. Men!

There was a routine set for the rest of the month. He dropped me off and sat and chatted with my family and had dinner and left. My family clearly liked the arrangement and so did I. After everything he had done for me, I thought. As soon as the month ended, the bodyguards were sent back and my dad paid for them. Surprisingly, Siddharth kept quiet. He then told me that the routine we had would be the same. They were not allowing me to travel alone for now. "Police's advisory," he said and my dad agreed. I sighed and said okay. It was extremely pleasant travelling with him and I was okay doing it. I didn't mention this to anyone.

I blossomed under his protection. I started singing along with the music at work and he was in a good mood throughout. We danced to the music and he sat and watched and then took me to a restaurant that had a dance floor.

"May I have this dance?" he said when we were sipping mocktails. I stood up and he extended his arm. We walked to the dance floor and danced imperfectly. But it was fun and we ended up laughing at ourselves. That set the tone for the future. Every time he took me out once a week, he asked my dad's permission and then asked me. I protested to my dad.

"He is a dear friend. He doesn't need permission."

Dad simply smiled and said, "To each his own."

My team started teasing me about him. "There is love in the air," they hummed. It didn't irritate him as it did me. "It's called friendship," I said and they protested.

He asked me, "Never been in love?" I shook my head and said, "No. I had my share of crushes, but not the real thing."

"I see. You will figure it out soon."

I told my mom what he had said and she smiled. "So what do you feel for him?" asked my mom. I asked her what she thought. She said, "What you think matters, Sia, not what everyone else thinks." I agreed and went to my room. I examined my feelings and it left me surprised. I had fallen for him. That was clear. I wanted to check if it was infatuation or the real thing.

The next day when he came to pick me up, I was conscious about my feelings and shyly looked away when he looked at me. He was ecstatic. He looked up at the skies and said, "Thank you, I owe you one."

My parents laughed at this. "And how do you plan to square it off?" my dad asked.

"By going for darshan with my family."

He looked at us. We agreed. "I need to check some things," I said and he agreed. "Take your time, But is it promising?"

"Yes," I said and went to sit in the car. I switched on the radio and pretended to listen to it. My heart was thudding and I planned to calm it down before he arrived. No such luck. He came before my nerves were in control, but thankfully said nothing.

By the time we reached our destination, My nerves were shot. He was amused. But kept quiet. When we got down from the car, I could see he had visitors. I excused myself and went to my team to discuss the day's work items. There were about 3 visitors, 2 women and Abhimanyu. I presumed one was his wife and had no idea about the second.

Siddharth was friendly with both the women. No attempt to touch or hug. His tone was different and he packed them off in a short time. I asked him who they were and he said Abhimanyu was his cousin from his mother's side and Rita was his wife, the other was Siddharth's ex. The one he proclaimed to be a bitch.

"Now that I am doing well, she wants me back," he said and I could feel tears pricking my eyes. He exclaimed and yanked me by the arm and hugged me. "So soft, Sia. What am I going to do with you? I wish I had an avatar that will stay with you all day. But alas we are mortals."

I wiped my face in the kerchief he handed me and I said, "Not you."

He grinned. "Nut," he said affectionately. "I love you." I absorbed the moment and said," Likewise, your highness." He burst out laughing and my team that had heard the conversation cheered us and yelled their best wishes.

We went home and he ordered sweets from a 5-star restaurant and we celebrated with old Hindi music in the background. "Now the family is complete," my dad said. I beamed at him. "When did you know, Dad?" I asked and he said, "From his first visit. He asked for your hand and then proceeded to discuss the criminals. He wanted a love match, so he asked for some time to make you fall in love with him. His was love at first sight."

I was astounded. "You knew it then?" Siddharth nodded and winked at me. I blushed. Everyone laughed. "Mom, I will cook tonight," said Siddharth to my mom. Mom agreed. She looked at my dad and he looked at Siddharth and said, "I am waiting." He said, "Thank you, Dad." My dad beamed.

"I need help with a girl at work," my brother said.

"Hear hear!" I said. "Talk to us. We are veterans at it."

My brother then showed some photographs and begged Siddharth for help. He took him to my room and they had a talk. Dad went up as well. I have never felt so cherished and loved in my life and I shared that with my mom. My mom warned me that Siddharth's relationship with his parents was not like ours. And she said now that you have taken a stand, you must stick to it in the face of adversities. I promised my mom I wouldn't run away and I would stand with Siddharth. The men in my life walked in then and Siddharth thanked my mom. They then proceeded to cook the best dinner anyone ever had.

What followed was the best week. He would bring flowers and spring them on me suddenly. We would dance to the music from his laptop in his villa and he would sit and gaze at me work and I would do the same. "The best time of my life," I told him and he said, "Likewise, my angel."

The beginning of the next Monday was like a slap on my face. Abhimanyu armed with two women came for a visit again to his villa and this time it was ugly. He said he had got a private investigator to check on Siddharth and Abhimanyu got a earful he said.

He told me that Vishaka was his betrothed and I had no chance of getting approval from his parents as Vishaka was his family's choice and more importantly I was a widow. Vishaka came close to me and tried to get a part of me to shake, But I sidestepped and warned her, "Don't you dare. I am a karate expert."

She backed down. With a whole lot of makeup, she looked downright evil. Same with the other 2. I wondered how I could have thought Abhimanyu was handsome. He was a parasite. I learned during the tirade that Siddharth was his meal ticket and he had stopped giving them alms. Vishaka was Rita's cousin. I finished connecting all the dots and told them, "I have work to do, which you will have no idea about," and left. Siddharth had a half-smile on his face. I pecked his cheek and went to work. He looked proud of me and said so. I smiled and went to my passions, which were him and his house.

Siddharth told them to leave his property and never to try to meet him or me again. They grudgingly left when he called his security, which he had beefed up when I was the target. This time I took care of him when he sat on the stairs. His work was done. I prepared a light snack which I read about recently – Paneer rolls - and he gobbled them up and refused to give it to anyone else. My team agreed and told me to be brave and handle the future side by side. I got their drift. We went home and he told my parents everything and then asked us if we wanted to hear his life story. We said, "Yes," in unison. He sat next to me and held my hand.

Siddharth's Story

My earliest memory is that of my mother beating me at the age of 6. It was ruthless and I had bruises on my upper body all the time. My dad had to go to work, so he came to know of this when he came back at night. He used to apply ointment on it and begged me to forgive him. He was working overtime only to send me to a residential school and it didn't happen soon. I was good at studies and getting admission was not the problem. Money was the problem, but my dad didn't relent. He found a good job that paid well and was determined to send me.

My mother used to pretend she didn't abuse me and pretended to love me in front of dad or any other relative. Initially, my dad was lured into this sham, but I wasn't. My dad had a piece of land, which he had bought 20 years back. He checked the value of it and he was very happy that day. He got the admission request papers from a reputed residential school and we both went for the interview. I bagged a seat.

My dad prepared all the items I needed to take with me and apologised to me about not sending homemade sweets. I said, "That's okay, Dad. What about you?"

"I go to work in the morning and come back at night," he said.

For now, we will leave it at that. So at age 12, I went to a residential school and stayed there even during holidays. I got some extra money from Dad. He worked to keep me in school and I will never forget that. That was his motivation. His marriage was in the doldrums.

In school, I was very good at academics. I enjoyed the classes and made some friends but none I could confide in. They came from stable upper-middle-class families and I was middle class. I became a loner with my background and brushed up on my intelligence with books in the library. At age 16, I developed a liking for sports and tried to qualify for cricket, but lost as I didn't have enough money for coaching. I made sure my dad didn't hear of it."

Sia squeezed my hand and I gave her a smile.

"The school was attached to a college and I got scholarships for B.Com and then MBA in strategy and I passed in the campus interview and I was selected with a good package to work for a multinational company. I was

24 by then, and have been earning since and making sure that my dad does not need anything. He is still married to my mother and I wonder why. We don't discuss things openly like this family does. I plan to keep him in good humour and wealth forever. If that means my mother accompanying him, so be it."

She looked at me and I agreed. "I will treat them well, my love," Sia said. "I know that," I said. "But I was worried about what my mother would do to you."

"After college, you came to Bangalore?" Sia's dad asked.

"Nope," I said. "I was in Chennai for my job for about 10 years and then changed my company last year. I am 34 years old and this company is very employee-friendly and I guess it was time to meet my destiny," I said and looked at her and the family.

"It was in Chennai my mother forced me to meet Vishaka about 4 years back and I disagreed to the betrothal. She wanted to meet for some time and then to make a decision. My dad was against it. He said, 'The plan is to get away from your mother's family, not get entangled in it. She is a vamp,' he said. They wanted me to get married to her so that the money I give to my mother increased and is distributed to them as it has been for 10 years. I knew about it but I didn't ask her anything. I pretty much don't talk to her. It's me and my dad. She comes with her sister and their family. I broke up with Vishaka after 2 meetings. She is mean through and through."

Back to Sia

My dad asked for his dad's number so that he could talk to him about the marriage and Siddharth readily gave it to him. "He will be in the park with friends. Why don't you call him tomorrow, Dad?" he said. "I will prepare him to expect it tonight."

My dad agreed and asked if he had concerns about me being a widow. Siddharth said no and showed the WhatsApp message from his dad. I grabbed it amidst laughter and read what he had said, 'I like her son, don't let her go. Whatever your mother and her family says.' I beamed and passed it on to Dad and Mom.

We ordered in Siddharth's favourite cuisine, Italian. My dad then asked Siddharth if he had any specific sentiment towards his rented accommodation and he said, "No, Dad, just a place to sleep."

"Bring your stuff here and occupy the guest room till your wedding," my dad said and I was ecstatic.

He said okay. "I will go with you," said my dad and they went and came with 2 kit bags. "Have you boarded your stuff anywhere?" I asked.

He smilingly said, "No sweetheart. This is it."

He explained that he always went for a furnished apartment and the villa was his first house. "Your wardrobe will be full soon," I said. I went with him to arrange the clothes he had and to have a look at them. "Good night, separate beds," Dad said. I blushed crimson and glared at my dad. He laughed it away. So did Siddharth.

The next day my dad called Siddharth's dad after our breakfast and they had a detailed discussion about our wedding. I was a Kannada brahmin and he was a Tamil Iyer and his parents stayed in Chennai. His dad said that as soon as the house was complete, they would shift there for good.

"I get pictures and video's of the house and it looks fab. I got a picture of Sia as well," he told my dad. "I couldn't be happier. But his mother is a different story," he said.

My dad said Siddharth had appraised us of the situation. "If his mom was there, I would like to speak to her," my dad said. His dad refused. "Anyway, she is sleeping. That's all she does these days. You will anyway meet her in Bangalore," he said. My dad agreed and said he hoped to meet them soon and handed the phone to Siddharth.

My dad asked me when the house would be complete. "It will take a month, Dad," I said.

"Okay, then we will arrange for the wedding as soon as the house is done."

He asked my mother, "Can you arrange a wedding in 1 month?"

My mother clapped her hands and said, "Watch me."

The next month flew past. On the one hand, the villa was getting along beautifully, and on the other hand, my wedding preparations. Siddharth and I both agreed that we would not inform our so-called relatives. It would be our close family and close friends, so in total, the number came to less than 50.

Accordingly, my parents were searching for kalyana mantapa, when my dad proclaimed we can go to a 4-star restaurant and book the hall there as well. That would solve the problem of food as well. Siddharth said, "But what about the cost? I will share the wedding expenses." My dad put his foot down. "When you beget a baby girl, you will understand," he said.

And they all looked at me and I blushed as if automatically and then there was laughter. I heaved a sigh and asked if I could share the expenses, the answer was NO.

The house was ready 2 days earlier than my estimation thanks to my team. Siddharth bundled my family in the car and proudly showed them around. The study now was bigger than the original plan as it had to seat me and my husband-to-be. My family thought it was fantastic. So did Siddharth. I said, "This is my best work ever."

"And your cheque?" Siddharth asked smilingly.

I glared at him. "This is my house."

He agreed hurriedly and hugged me and looked at me keenly. I smiled and he was okay with it. His parents were arriving in the evening. Siddharth had to go to the airport. So we left in a cab to my dad's home.

He later told me that he was shocked at my mother's appearance when he saw her. He last saw them 6 months back. We went to visit his parents the next day and I understood what he told me on the phone the previous day. I had warned the family. My parents paid their respects to them and called me. I touched their feet and heard a staccato near my to-be-mother-in-law. She stepped back.

My father-in-law blessed me and apologised for his wife. My parents and his father sat down to discuss the wedding schedule the next day and he was happy with the preparations. "Siddharth is a gem of a boy," his father said and my parents agreed.

"So is your daughter. She has done a great job on the house," he said and I was very very happy.

The wedding the next day went on in a beautiful and phased manner. The hotel co-operated fully and the function was a success and I became Sia Siddharth. I said it to myself a couple of times and he grinned and said, "Mine."

I was thrilled but his mother's demeanour worried me. I told my mom, "I think she has a earpiece and she is talking to someone or someone is talking to her."

My mother said, "Unless you are sure, don't mention it to anyone except me and your dad."

I got her drift. I said I would follow her advice.

We decided to postpone our honeymoon till our house was adequately staffed and his dad was on his feet.

This meant a quick visit from my father-in-law Naresh to Chennai to close some accounts and transfer the rest here in Bangalore. Siddharth said he would accompany his dad and I was fine with it. I wanted to keep an eye on my mother-in-law.

My husband knew I was distracted and asked me the reason worriedly. "I am a married woman," I told him. "And with it comes some responsibilities." He wanted to know what. I promised him that when he came back from his 2-day trip, I would tell him everything. My dad sent Sharath to stay with us for the 2 days. He plonked himself in the minitheatre in the basement and gorged on movies.

My mother-in-law Padma got up the next day at about 11 AM and looked around to see if anyone was watching. I grabbed my phone and slowly followed her and saw her stand in the midst of the garden, which was not visible from the entrance. She took out a syringe from under her saree and pricked her forearm. I was shocked but had the presence of mind to take a video of it and left and came back to my house.

She saw where I was and spoke under her breath, "She is in the hall," and went to her room. I went down to the amphitheatre and told my brother everything. He said he would step outside the house and call our parents and inform them. I went back to the hall and sat working on a piecemeal assignment I had got. She went back to her room after peeping at me and shut the door. I drew a long breath and let the tears flow. Sharath came back and said my dad would talk to my husband and his dad ASAP. I cooked and we had it. Padma took it to her room and said she didn't want to eat it in a widow's presence. She would be doomed, she said. I said , "I had cooked it. Surely that must mean something."

She glared at me and shouted, "She talks back to me, so do something to her soon," and banged her door along with the food.

In the evening at around 7, my brother had a call and I told him to take it in my office. I sat alone in the drawing-room and Padma came out and asked me if I could take her for a walk outside. She was fed up of being cooped outside. I knew it was a ruse, but went with her anyway. I yelled to my brother that we were going for a walk. He gave me a thumbs up. I went with her and asked her if there was a specific place she wanted to go to. She said she wanted to go to the road and see if the other houses were built or not.

We walked towards the road and after we passed security, suddenly we came upon her sister and her family. There were some paid thugs as well and they had assembled a wooden pyre and it was flaming. Abhimanyu yelled, "This is your rightful place, you widow. How dare you put a spanner in our works."

They started dragging me to the pyre and I yelled for Sharath and dialled quick dial which had Siddharth and my dad in it.

My phone was ripped from my arm and thrown in the fire. It gobbled it up. My security was looking at us from afar and trying to decipher what was happening. I was about 2 feet from the pyre when I was freed abruptly and all the men in my family threw a punch at them. Our security had already called the police and they arrived on the spot and arrested all of them. They asked me if my mother in law was involved. I said, "No. I will come to the police station tomorrow with proof that she was being used by her sister Manorama and her family."

Siddharth pulled me into his arms and I burst out weeping. He carried me to the house and everyone trooped in. His dad thanked the security and we went inside and sat in the drawing-room. When we both had finished weeping my dad asked me gently, "You said you had some proof, princess. Where is it?" I said it was on my phone and they threw my phone into the pyre.

"You sent it to me to send it to dad and Siddharth, Sia," my brother said and they all looked at the video that I had sent. "Drugs," both Siddharth and his dad proclaimed.

"All these years? I don't know, but it appears that she was being blackmailed. They can see everything through her and she takes direction from them," I said. His dad said he would check her. She had gone to her room as soon as we came back.

Siddharth went and stood outside. He refused to let me be with him. "No. you have done enough," he said and again teared up.

"Forgive me?" he said and I smiled at him. He calmed down. Naresh found the earpiece and the injections she had saved in her clothing. He took photographs and then asked us whether he should remove it or not. Siddharth called the police and asked the question.

"They said do it with the video on so that they can see it."

This was carried out and they asked Siddharth and his family to pay a visit to the police station to record our statements. "Get a lawyer," the inspector said and Siddharth called the same lawyer that my dad had used for me. He said he would come over.

Siddharth and Naresh woke up Padma and got her to the drawing-room. They asked her to tell all of us what happened to her. Padma answered that she was on drugs for the past 20 years, Siddharth corrected her, "28 years."

"Yes around that," she said. Initially, it was tablets and they made her do things for it. Then when Siddharth was gainfully employed, they started asking for money. She told Siddharth, "Whatever you gave me, I handed over to them. Now that you said you will stop it as you came to know that I was giving it to them, they panicked and decided to attack Sia. I was to have a microphone in my ear and a camera in my blouse so that they are aware of what was happening. This started when Siddharth had banned them from his property."

The lawyer had also come and he listened to the story. Siddharth and Naresh were still in shock. Mom made some tea for everyone and I said I would prepare dinner, but my husband refused to let me go. My mom said she would do it. Siddharth asked Sharath to stay with her in the kitchen till Mom was done. Mom put her hand on Siddharth's head and tousled it. "They are gone, lad."

He replied, "No, mama. Not till we are completely sure that they don't have accomplices. What about the suppliers of drugs?" He asked dad if they could all move in so that we were safe in one place. My dad and his dad agreed to the plan.

"We will go tomorrow and get our stuff," Dad said.

His dad was telling my dad about his point of view.

After Siddharth was born, there were light tantrums," Naresh said. "Then at the age of 6, beating the child started. I think we have to record from there."

The lawyer agreed. Naresh said he left for work in the morning and came home at night. He was holding 2 jobs as he wanted to send Siddharth to the best school. "And he didn't disappoint me," he said.

He also said that Padma was initially a good soul and he kept that memory and stayed with her. He knew they came in his absence and abused her verbally because Siddharth had told him about it. Then we both lost interest in her and I just stayed together but I came home only to sleep. "We had separate rooms after Siddharth left for his residential school," he said.

I said, "We have to put Amma in a rehab."

Siddharth asked the lawyer what our next steps were. He said we had to tell all of this to the police and ask their permission to put Padma in the rehab centre. "I suggest we go to the police station now," he said. He and his mom and dad along with the lawyer went to the police station after asking the security to move up to the house. Siddharth thanked them and said they did fab work and he was grateful.

Later, Siddharth told me that his mom told the police everything and then asked them for drugs. The police inspector said, "She has to be admitted ASAP," and gave the address of 2 de-addiction centers. He also said, "If the criminals gave a counter-complaint, we will have to get Padma from the rehab to the court, otherwise it was closed."

They had the proof and had recorded her statement and that should be enough. Siddharth asked the police about the drug cartel and he was informed that they have received a lead and would be conducting the raid the following day. "We will inform you," the inspector said.

From the police station, they went to different de-addiction centres and saw their facilities and Siddharth chose the best one and they admitted her there and came home. We had dinner waiting. All of us sat in the drawing-room and my dad put on some music and we had some food. Everyone retired to their rooms and Siddharth checked if the security had changed for the night. It was and he spoke to them and appraised them of the situation and then came indoors after locking the main door.

He then carried me upstairs to our room and laid me gently on the bed. We looked at each other and said, "I love you," in unison. I grabbed him and hugged him and went to sleep.

Epilogue

Padma stayed in rehab for nearly a year and then came out to stay with Sia and Siddharth. Sia took care of her visits to the doctor and tablets on time along with Naresh.

Siddharth was second in line to the top job in a year's time

Sia was pregnant after a year and she gave birth to twins, a boy and a girl. Siddharth was over the moon.

Maya's Journey

I sat in my seat in the courtroom to absorb the verdict. I have won my first case, I thought. I looked at my guardian, Santosh and smiled and mouthed a 'thank you'. He waved it away and said, "My child." I said, "Yes."

Santhosh motioned me towards the opposing counsel. I got up and shook hands with him. Rishabh was my co-counsel and he hugged me to my surprise. I hugged him back. Santhosh noted it and smiled happily. He said, "Maya, I am going to a client's place for a meeting. Rishabh will drop you to the office. He is going there as well." I nodded my head.

Rishabh, aged 30 was Santhosh's blue-eyed boy. He was a lawyer that fought tooth and nail for his client. Santhosh's firm was one of the best legal firms in the country. And I was his godchild. My mother, Sagarika, before passing on had made him promise that he would take care of me and that he was my guardian. He had told me plenty of times that he was blessed by my maternal grandfather and that was why he was able to steer his firm to the top position.

The blessing was my custody. I was curious to know about my mother and my grandfather's lives, especially with my dad as he was surpassed by both of them. Santhosh had kept that part of their lives in the dark. I asked him, "Now?"

He said, "In a short while." I asked him if I was ready to hear about their lives after each milestone and he had said, "Not yet," so far. I smiled. "Thanks, Dad." He went to his destination happy. He had not insisted I call him anything, But he was my father through his actions and I was proud to be called his daughter by merit.

Rishabh said he was ready to leave for our office if I was. I nodded and we went to his car. I had to ask Dad if I could learn to drive a car. I wanted to be a daughter he was proud of and I felt mobility was important. "Do you want to learn how to drive?" Rishabh asked and I replied in the affirmative. "I will ask Santhosh sir," he said. "Me too," I said. "I will teach you," he said and that was it. I was zapped.

He didn't ask me, I thought but I was pleased so I kept quiet. I thought Rishabh was strong and powerful. He had joined the firm 5 years back and was on a career path that many aspired to. I had a crush on him for his behaviour and his work. I had much to learn from him. I hoped Dad would allow it. We reached the office 15 minutes later and I was greeted with congrats and well dones by my colleagues. There were sweets and it was a happy atmosphere. I thought I should thank Dad for this as well. When I was little, I used to accompany Dad to this office and the old-timers thought of me as a child and the celebrations were genuine. I loved this office. I was given a list of cases that the firm was fighting and who was the counsel and my name appeared a couple of times. I was excited. I went to my bay and sat down to prepare. I was extremely happy.

Rishabh came and pulled a chair and sat next to me and said I was his co-counsel in one case and he needed some details that I should get ready by the end of the day. I noted it down and started work. He went to his cabin and I was able to focus on work. Dad came to the office in the afternoon and called me in. I went with a pad and pen. As anticipated, he had some data to give me and said I was his co-counsel for the other case and he needed me to work on the opening statement and work on some details from the client.

He said I could call them and say I was from 'Sabarwal and co' and they would agree to the meeting. I was raring to go. "Thanks for the sweets, Dad," I said and he replied, "Not me, child. It was Rishabh." I was surprised.

He looked at the paper lying on his desk and laughed and passed it on to me. It was an application to teach me to drive from Rishabh. I was pleased and asked, "Dad, can I ?" He said, "Most definitely. Why don't we buy a car and you can learn driving? That way there will be no time wasted in trying to adjust." I agreed and asked, "From the fund?"

He disagreed, "No, my gift."

"Okay, Dad. Thank you," I said.

"So I can do this?" he asked.

"Yes," I said.

"Good. I have plans," he said pleased.

He wrote 'going to buy a car for Maya this Saturday. Care to come along?' on the application from Rishabh. and I took it with me to place it on Rishabh's desk. He was in his cabin and I gave it to him. He said he was in the process of shortlisting cars and asked me if I knew the budget. "No idea," I said. "Dad's gift."

"Okay," he said. "I will talk to him."

The week went very well for me. I was preparing the details for the cases that I had been assigned. I learnt the intricacies of the cases and the laws that governed it. Both Rishabh and Santhosh were very good leaders and I learnt the art of managing the client's expectations from them as well. It was an art, 'How to handle your client'.

I had also googled some cars and checked the prices as well. So when Saturday came, I was prepared to shop for my car with the men. I stayed in Dad's house ever since I was born and Rishabh joined us at our house and we went to the showrooms and test drove some cars before both of them agreed on the output. I lost them when they started discussing the kms and made a mental note to learn some car jargon. I picked the car that appealed to me after their shortlist. Rishabh drove it to my house and I went back with Dad in his car.

I was excited about the entire day. Rishabh showed a keen interest in my point of view and helped me to understand the focal points and the mechanics before he got into the debate about them with dad. He was going to be teaching me driving from Monday in the morning at 6 AM. He said one hour was enough every day and I agreed. Rishabh stayed on for dinner and left soon after. Dad told me that Rishabh had lost both his parents last year one by one and he stayed alone in a flat in an upscale area. "He should be thinking of getting married soon," Dad said. I drew a sharp breath in and Dad noticed it but didn't mention it, so I let it pass. I have a crush on Rishabh, so this reaction is normal, I told myself.

On Monday morning, I was ready at 6 AM and Rishabh was right on time. We went with Dad's blessing to a secluded place for my first class. The one hour went by speedily and I was as clumsy as ever and upset with myself. Rishabh tried to make me feel better by saying the first two days are the most difficult and then the learning starts. But I was feeling like the biggest loser and plonked myself in a chair opposite Dad and told him his daughter could never learn how to drive a car. He poured both of us tea and we had it.

"It's the learning curve. All of us have been in that place. It's perfectly normal," he said. They both smiled and reminisced about their driving experience. "It becomes second nature after learning," Sathosh said. I felt better after their stories and got up to go to my room to get ready.

Rishabh left to do the same. I wore western formals to office and I thought it suited me.

We met in the office and Rishabh asked, "Don't you wear Indian?" I said, "Sometimes, but I prefer western to work."

"Why?" he asked. "Why?" I repeated. "I guess I like it more."

"Yes, but why?"

"It looks professional," I said.

He persisted, "Have you tried cottons?"

"No," I said.

"Let me take you to a store I like," he said.

"When?' I asked."

"How about this evening? I will drop you home," he said.

"That would be fine," I said and went to my desk.

That felt like an interrogation. Mild by his standards. I was amused when I thought about it. The day breezed by and I told Dad that Rishabh was taking me shopping. "Most interesting," he said and asked him to have dinner with us. "Our cook will whip up something," he said and he asked Rishabh what cuisine he liked.

Rishabh said, "South Indian," and I thought it must be because he was a North Indian. I liked North Indian.

He took me to a cotton paradise, It had every garment in cotton and for every occasion. I was impressed. He picked a couple of salwar suits and some churidars and I was impressed by his selection and asked to try them. He insisted that I show him the dress and I did a mini catwalk for him and he okayed my purchases. I picked workwear and a couple of sarees.

"I need help with sarees," I confided in him. "I don't know who to ask for help. I am a quick learner except when it comes to cars," I said.

He said he would ask Shreya, in the office to help me.

"Oh. Will she do it ?: I asked.

"Most certainly. I will pick her from work and drop her to your house and drop her home. Leave it to me. You can also look it up online," he suggested.

I said, "I will do that."

Once I was done and he was satisfied, he dropped me home and got into a work discussion with Dad. I quickly dropped my purchases in my room and ran back as I didn't want to miss it. Dad exclaimed, "You didn't show it to me."

I went back and showed him my new Indian wardrobe. He had his favourites and said, "Your mom used to look like a goddess in a saree." I don't know if he said it deliberately or it was a slip, as he never spoke about my family to me. I froze and asked him if he had a photo.

"Most certainly," he said and gave me the album from his desk drawer.

I took a deep breath and opened it. Rishabh sat next to me and we saw the pictures of my grandparents and my mother. It didn't have pictures of my dad. It had my childhood pictures and Rishabh was interested in them. "This is for you," Dad said motioning to the album. I thanked him and asked him, "Soon?"

He said, "Yes," and patted my head. Rishabh asked, What?"

"He will tell me about my family and the goings-on soon to me," I responded.

"Why, sir?" he asked.

"I wanted her to reach a stage maturity-wise before telling her the story," responded Santhosh. "It is a tough story to digest.

"She knows me and she trusts me," he said. "Can I listen with her whenever you think it is the right time?" Rishabh asked.

"You should ask Maya the question," Dad said.

"I will, soon," he said and left it at that.

They both smiled at each other and that was that. I was still gazing at my mother's picture and wondering what she had been through. "Sometimes the waiting is more painful," Rishabh said.

"No," countered Santhosh.

Rishabh said, "I will be there."

"Let's see," said Santhosh.

Dinner was a 3-course meal in the south Indian style and it was very good. We dug in and Rishabh left soon after. "Tomorrow at 6 AM," he said and left. I was reminded of the ordeal before me and okayed the reminder. This became the routine for the next few days. I stopped getting confused and started understanding the mechanics of a car. I was a good learner according to Rishabh, but he was biased. It was apparent that he liked me, but since he had said nothing, I kept quiet as well. He brought Shreya home one day and I was excited. I had by then done the online coaching and she showed me how to drape a saree and I did it. Dad said he wanted to see me in a saree. And I did the draping with Sherya's help and went down to show Dad and Rishabh.

They had kept the camera's ready and Shreya was delighted as well. They took pictures of me alone and with each one of them. It was like a homecoming.

"You look like your mother," Santhosh said and he teared up.

"Dad," I said and hugged him.

Rishabh said I looked like an angel and I should wear it often. Shreya was happy she got to be a part of this happiness and said so too. Dad invited her to dinner and she accepted. Rishabh dropped her home after dinner and went home.

Both the cases that I was a part of came one after the other to the courtroom and I got to open with dad in one case and interrogate in the other case with Rishabh. We won both and they said it was because of the work I had put in. "The background work was fantastic," Rishabh said and I beamed. Dad looked amused most of the time when we both were present. I knew my relationship with Rishabh was drawing smiles in the office and I kept quiet about it. No one asked me directly, but Rishabh was teased about it. He said on the day I passed the test on my driving, he had something to tell me and I thought I knew what it was but still, my heart pounded suddenly. I knew Dad approved, so no problems there. Everybody knew Dad approved when he deferred the decision about my work to Rishabh and said, "He has the right."

Rishabh was in the line to be made partner. There were 2 partners now. Santhosh and his best friend Sundar. There were about 6 senior lawyers (including the partners) in all and 10 junior lawyers and the back office personnel in the office. It was called Sabarwal, which was Santhosh's last name and co. Rishabh was made partner amid loud cheering and fanfare in the office. The paperwork was done soon. He was selected because of his track record which was the criteria. The other 3 senior lawyers said, "Watch out, Rishabh. We are in the line as well."

Rishabh laughed and said, "The more, the merrier."

"That's true," Dad said. "I am looking forward to that day," he declared.

I made him a sketch of him with a crown and sitting on the throne and left it on his desk. He laughed when he saw it. And said, "The place next to me is empty," and I smiled amid thundering in my ear. He said, "Thank you," and left.

Dad yelled for me from his cabin. He asked why he never received a sketch. "It is ready," I said.

I had made a picture of him holding hands with my mom. It was in my drawer and I handed it to him. He teared up and said it was the most beautiful gift anyone had given him. Rishabh barged into his office and asked to see it. Santhosh handed it over and he asked, "Is she right?" and Santhosh nodded and I smiled.

"I can now hear the story, Dad," I said and left to go to my bay. Rishabh stayed on and had a brief conversation with Dad and he left his cabin with a smile as well. "Good perception," he noted. "So about us…" I smiled and nodded. He laughed and went to his cabin.

That evening Dad had a framed picture of my mother and the sketch framed as well and he hung it in the drawing-room. "My dear child, your mom told me that if there is a way, she would most definitely come back as your child and made me promise that I will take good care of her then. I hope you will stay in the same city as me. If not, I plan to visit often," he said.

I said, "I am not leaving the house, Dad. This is my house and he will have to come and stay here. I will tell him," I said and dad laughed. "Tell whom?"

Rishabh rang the doorbell. "Him," I said and Santhosh was filled with glee and said, "I will have to change the nameplate then. I will look for them on the internet."

Rishabh looked at him quizzically. "Between the 2 of you. I am an old man who is happy," he said and went to check if dinner was ready.

Rishabh asked me what the matter was and I said, "After marriage, my husband should come and stay here. I am not leaving dad," I said. "He wants to take care of my children as he sees mom in them." I looked at him questioningly and he appeared amused.

"Anything else?"

"Not now," I said.

"The wily old man," he said and looked at him when he came back singing a song.

"Well?" he looked at Rishabh questioningly. He nodded his head and Dad put on Elvis Presley songs and got me up to dance with him. I dragged Rishabh and the 3 of us danced our hearts out.

In the course of the song, Rishabh went down on his knees and proposed to me. I accepted and Santhosh opened a champagne bottle to celebrate the occasion. Since he had drunk alcohol, Rishabh decided to stay the night instead of leaving for his house.

The next morning, we took the car to his house and he showered and changed and went back home to collect his car. I was more confident now regarding car driving. Rishabh had all his meals with dad and me and I learnt his likes and dislikes as I had started instructing the cook regarding the dishes to make. I wanted to learn cooking as well. That day, the office wore a celebratory look with sweets and juices and some sandwiches doing the rounds. This time it was Dad. He announced that Rishabh and I would be getting married soon. We were congratulated by everyone in the office and we all got down to work. Dad called me and Rishabh to his cabin and said. "After your honeymoon. I promise."

We both looked at each other and I said, "Thank you, Dad."

He passed on a file to me. It was the fund details that my grandparents had left me. I knew about it and it was 10 crores. This was news. "The details of the past 25 years are there. You are now capable of handling it on your own. Both of you," he said.

I did a quick look and said, "Dad the money has multiplied."

"Good investments," said Rishabh after looking at the file. "And no outflows,"

He grinned at Santhosh. I looked at dad and said, "Dad! All this while you used to say there is a fund."

"And I was not wrong," he declared.

"There is a fund. After marriage, you will be my responsibility and you are also earning. I want to spend my money," said Rishabh.

"And I will arrange the wedding," Santhosh said and they both looked at me.

I said okay to both and went to my bay with the file. When Rishabh came out, I asked him. "We will keep it for our children. My children. I will spend. Do you know how much I get compensated as a partner?" he asked I said I had an idea.

"We will gift it to them after they have settled," he said and asked, "2 children, please?"

I agreed since we were both only children. I was curious about having a sibling. Dad came out and said, "I heard children discussed."

"Is there a bug here?" I asked.

He said, "No, I was passing by. Once the first child comes to us, I will retire. I want to spend as much time as I can with them. That's my career plan."

Rishabh was stunned. "But that could happen in maybe a year's time. You have about 4 cases if I am not mistaken."

"I have juniors and Sundar covers for me always. Why do you think I am not taking any new cases?"

He left us and went to his cabin singing. He had started playing music in his cabin. Sundar yelled from across the floor, "So the day has come, you rascal. I thought I would beat you to it. But no such luck," he said.

Dad said, "I am unbeatable," and they burst out singing the song playing in his cabin. Everyone laughed out loud. It was beginning of the festivities and everyone pitched in and I was the centre of attention along with Rishabh.

We wanted a simple wedding and so Dad called the office and a couple of his close friends and so did Rishabh and I. We got married amidst good souls. We had planned on a Goa getaway for 4 days and then it was back to work. Dad looked at Rishabh when we were about to leave and told Rishabh, "Don't leave her alone. Even for a second."

Rishabh nodded and I said, "Even now?"

"Especially now," he said. "I have arranged for bodyguards. They won't infringe on your privacy." We agreed and left after Rishabh spoke to them.

"This is a good idea," Rishabh said on the flight. "We are in this profession and dealing with criminals day in and out and I think this is a fab idea," he declared.

"I have had bodyguards for as long as I remember," I said. "School, college and law college. Only now, it was removed because I had entered Dad's world and he or you were always with me. I was surprised when he agreed to my car driving," I said. "I would like to know his reasoning."

Rishabh got the picture. "He is guarding me against my biological father," I told him.

"Yeah," he said. "I guessed as much."

I need to have a long conversation with Dad," he said. "We have to do the same for our children. He is fighting cases against him. They fight tooth and nail and Dad has won some and lost a few."

"But this will go on till he dies," I said. I wish it happens soon. I am heartily sick of him. Dad had his group of best friends who helped him with me. He doesn't trust anyone except them and now you,."

Rishabh was listening carefully while keeping an eye on what was happening around us. "Do you mind?" I asked him. He hugged me and said, "Not at all. Dad has grown in stature in my eyes," he said.

We reached Goa and we went to our resort and had the most wonderful holiday of my life. I fell even more in love with my husband and Rishabh said he never knew his wife had such a wonderful sense of humour. He gave me gifts at every beautiful moment we spent and I was feeling cherished and loved in his presence. We went back to Bangalore in high spirits. Dad was at the airport to receive us. Rishabh and I had two more days of leave as did Santhosh.

We went home and Rishabh paused in the doorway to take in the new nameplate which had his name, then mine and then Santhosh's. "I will retire soon," Dad said. We went in and told him about Goa and he smiled and wished he didn't have to tell us the story and spoil our mood. But we had to do it. So we came and sat in the drawing-room and waited for Santhosh to arrive. He came with an old diary and gave it to me.

"That's your mother's. Read it. I am here for questions."

We both read it together. It was an account by Sagarika, my mother.

Sagarika's Story

I think I have fallen in love with Ganesh. He is a nice guy with a humble background and I can't help falling in love with him. He has agreed to stay with Mom and Dad after our wedding. I hope Dad agrees to this match.

Dad disagreed with my choice of husband. He said he has someone else in mind. I am crushed. Ganesh suggested that we get married in secret and then tell my Dad and Mom, that way they have no option but to agree. More so, if we beget a child.

I went along with Ganesh's plan and we got married in the temple and registered it with the registrar office. Ganesh suggested we go to his place in Kolkata for a few days and then come back and visit my parents

I agreed.

Ganesh slapped me today. I am still in shock. He didn't apologise. I am all alone here and no one will know what had happened to me. I am scared.

Ganesh has taken to beating me every day. It is a daily affair now.

Every time you raise your hand to hit me,

Pause and think

What if someone did the same to you?

For this is violation and subjudication.

Every time you remove your belt to beat me,

Pause and think

What if someone did the same to you?

I wish someone does and I am there to witness it.

I tried to get in touch with Dad today without Ganesh's knowledge. The line was bad but Dad said he will send someone ASAP.

Two bodyguards came to my house when Ganesh was away and showed me their IDs. Dad had sent them to bring me to Bangalore safe and sound. I was relieved and left with them. Dad was furious with my tale and he contacted his lawyer, Santhosh and asked me to divorce him. I agreed.

I got my divorce because of domestic violence and the lawyer was very good. Dad said he was whom I had in mind for you. He just said that he was ready to marry you whenever you were ready.

I had to heal first my mom said to Santhosh and he agreed. He came and spent about 30 minutes every day with me. I started enjoying the experience.

I am pregnant. I told Santhosh first and he welcomed the baby. He filed a petition in the court that my ex-husband has no claim on the child. I testified again in court about the violent side of Ganesh and the court agreed to grant the plea.

Santhosh asked me to marry him, and in the interest of the baby and I, Dad and Mom agreed to it and so did I.

Today I married Santhosh. I hope this time I am proven lucky.

It has been 3 months after my marriage to Santhosh and Dad has been proven right. Santhosh is a doting husband and I plan to ask him to adopt my child. My baby will be safe in his protection.

I delivered and it is a baby girl. Santhosh is smitten with the baby and I asked him to adopt Maya and he readily agreed.

Adoption is done. I couldn't be happier.

I am diagnosed with cancer. It is in the 3rd stage.

I'm happy my daughter's life is in safe hands.

Sorry, Santhosh. I am leaving you so soon. We had so many experiences to fulfil.

Back to Maya

Rishabh asked abruptly, "Did he rape her?" Santhosh nodded his head. He was weeping, so were we.

"I made it my mission to screw him uptight and have been doing my best for 25 years with my friends," Dad said.

"Dad, can I see the cases so far?" I asked him. He handed the file to me. Rishabh took it from me and said, "I am in this from now on."

"Me too," I said.

"Yes to Rishabh and 'no' to Maya," he said.

"Why dad?" we both asked.

"He will be there and I don't want him even looking at my child," he said. 'I promised Sagarika. I am answerable to her. We have promised to meet in the other world."

"I agree with Dad," Rishabh said.

The 3 of us sat in the drawing-room and dad recounted the beautiful times he shared with his wife. "It was the most beautiful time I shared with your mother," he said. And Rishabh wanted to know how he managed work and raised a child so effortlessly.

"I used to take her to the office and one of my friend's wives used to visit and take care of Maya and we used to work. Then school. I miss those days. We would rush back to the office to see Maya. You both have seen the pictures. She was a slightly plump kid and very very beautiful. My stress would evaporate when I came back and saw her. For all of us. It's the same even now," Dad said. "Raising a child is the most rewarding experience in one's life." "We can't wait," we said in unison.

My life with Rishabh was turning out to be the most beautiful time of my life. Just like Dad described his life with Mom. I told him and he agreed with me. "I am addicted to you," he said.

My biological dad was getting out of prison and Dad increased the security around me and I was never left alone by Rishabh and Dad. They took turns staying with me, even in the office. I was used to it and so I was fine. I enjoyed their company.

I thought I missed my period because of all the excitement in my life, But when it happened the second time, I bought a 'check at home' kit and it tested positive. I told Rishabh and he was ecstatic. We both decided we would get the test done in a hospital and then tell Dad. And that turned out to be positive.

"I am pregnant," I told Dad. "Someone has kept her promise to the love of her life."

Dad got it. I showed him the report and he was extremely excited and happy. He gave me the do's and don't's, from the book he had. "This what we did when your mom was expecting you," he said and I promised him I would follow the instructions.

Dad distributed sweets at the office and told them that he would retire in about 4 month's time. I got it. When I would be home most of the time. His friends came to the office and Rishabh got mocktails and it was an enjoyable day at work. I was pampered to the core by the men in my life and by my dear friends at work.

Dad and Rishabh and Dad's friends took Ganesh by the scruff of the neck and got him back to prison. They busted the gang that had employed him and rounded everyone and he went back for a short time. I thought, if only he went forever.

I asked them in their conference room whether he had ever threatened anyone with an attempt to murder. Now that my child was coming to us, I felt slightly scared for his/her safety. I now got how Dad felt about me. Same with Rishabh. Rishabh said, "Dad, we will protect them, won't we?"

"Yes, son," Dad said. "We are here and we have had plenty of practice."

"Yes," Rishabh said and his face cleared. "Why don't we go on the offensive and plant devices in his house and see where it takes us This was something that they had not done before. I will go and plant it," he said.

"No, we have good investigators and they will do it," Dad said. "They have been with us for 25 years, they are as old as Maya is," he said.

They started planning for it and I thought this will be the end of Dad's nemesis. I went out to my bay to finish my work as instructed by Rishabh. He came out to my desk and said, "I will learn from Dad and do my best protecting you and the baby. I promise," he said.

I gave him a smile. "I know," I said and we hugged.

The plant was done and Rishabh and Dad were constantly checking the reports and waiting. I didn't get too much into the details of checking the report as I felt the baby would be impacted. I surrounded myself with good memories and good music. Rishabh and Dad were relieved. I went to the office till I was 7 months pregnant and then worked from home for the next 2 months.

Dad was home after retirement by then and Rishabh was relieved and was able to focus on work because I would be safe in Dad's presence. About 2 days before my due date, I developed pains and Dad admitted me to the hospital and protected the hospital. I delivered the next day and it was a normal delivery. We were blessed with a baby girl. I smiled at Rishabh and looked at Dad. He was weeping silently. Rishabh hugged him. "She kept her promise to you, Dad," he said and Dad nodded his head. "What will we call her, Dad," Rishabh asked. "Samyukta," Dad said. "That was going to be our child's name."

"Samyukta," Rishabh and I parroted and looked at the tiny angel that had brought so much joy to our household.

"I have applied for paternity leave of 1 week," said Rishabh. Dad said, "Sundar has recommended 1-month leave from office but work from home for you," Dad said. "I will take it," he said.

"Okay. We need to make the house safe for the child. I will make a list and you get it done ASAP," Dad said. Rishabh agreed. They got the carpenter and did the closing with planks, which worked as blocks for the child's safety. They got the switchboards closed and there was a stop to the stairs.

Then they went shopping for my daughter's clothes and play items and the house was full of them. "Rishabh is responsible for the mini skirts," Dad said to me and I said, "When she grows up and wants it, he will be the first to oppose it." I laughed. Rishabh grinned. "I will show her photographs of this," he said. Nursery rhymes were the music we played after Samyukta's entry into our life and Dad played his favourites.

Rishabh was put in charge of their hunt against Ganesh as it was his idea and they were close to nailing him. Rishabh worked on the sting with him and sent a couple of investigators as his patrons and got him to admit to his escapades. He got it video recorded and they got the group that worked with him and he and his group were awarded life sentences. Rishabh got Dad's favourite brand of whiskey and invited Dad's close friends and their family and the investigators and we had a party in which Samyukta was the centre of attention. And she loved it, if all the happy shrieks were anything to go by.

Dad told me that my dear husband had said that some protection will always be there for our family and would I be okay with it. I agreed. "Good," Dad said. "I cannot let them all go." "Dad, I agree," I said. "And I understand," I said motioning to our precious little one. Dad smiled and said, "You are the most understanding daughter ever."

Dad looked after me and Samyukta and Rishabh looked after the firm. It grew from strength to strength and now there were 4 partners in total and they handled the expansion very well. Dad danced, pranced and walked on all fours with the baby on his back all around the house and became Samyukta's best friend. I enjoyed the time with them and joined office after 6 months. I started taking cases and worked with gusto. After about 2 months of my re-joining the firm, we got the news that Ganesh had died in jail after a brawl in prison.

Epilogue

Maya got pregnant for the second time after 3 years, Samyukta was in school by then.

Maya delivered a baby boy. Their family was complete.

A Blast from the Past

Iwalked the ramp at the climax of the fashion show amidst applause. I congratulated myself and went to meet my colleagues. "Congrats, Shradda," was everywhere dipped with sweetness and venom. I grimaced inside and air-kissed the colleagues but not one friend. I was called by my company's partner to be a part of a discussion with the buyers. I excused myself and went to do my job. It was quite late by the time we wrapped up business, but I had a car and a driver who worked as per my schedule, so I called the driver. Arun and waited in the foyer till he showed up with my car. If my work had to go on so late, I asked Arun to drop me off and take the car with him to his residence, or else there would be no transport for him. This arrangement worked well for both of us.

He dropped me off and waited until I walked inside the gate and then went to his house. I was exhausted. The work for this show had gone on for 3 months and today was the culmination, which was a grand success. I had taken a week off after the show and other than taking important calls, I could take the time to recuperate.

I went home, which was a 3 bedroom apartment in an upper-scale neighbourhood and it was expensive when I bought it. I could afford it and it was well protected by the security. I suddenly realised, I was hungry and so headed to the well-equipped kitchen. I loved to cook but since I was tired, I made some noodles and had them. Then I went to the bedroom and fell into my bed.

I had left a message for my elder sister who lived in Pune. So that was covered. She was the only living relative that I acknowledged. My father had passed on 2 years back and my mother had abandoned us, so we didn't consider her a part of our family.

I got up at 11 AM the next day and looked at my messages on the phone. It was filled with best wishes and congrats messages for the show. I then came across Dhruva's message asking me the best time and day for lunch together. He had said, 'You are all over the supplement papers and it was a pleasure to know a celebrity'. I quickly messaged him a thank you, and asked him if tomorrow was okay for lunch.

My dear older sister had sent a message to call whenever I was free. She lived with her husband and 2 kids. So the best time for her was between 11 AM and 3 PM. I messaged her saying I would call in 2 day's time. I had something to eat. I had stocked up on fruits. I then went back to sleep after putting on Beethoven. I got up in the evening. I had some tea and sat in the balcony overlooking the garden of my apartment complex. I examined my feelings and found that I was content.

I was 32 years old and had 5 shows so far. One a year and they were all successful. The clothes were picked up in record time and I then focussed on the next show. Happiness had disappeared and contentment took its place. It's about time I focussed on my personal life, I thought. I had achieved whatever I wanted to. My own label. A good company to work for and a fat bank balance and my own property.

Now I need a family of my own. The biological clock was also ticking. With a frown, I thought of Dhruva, an eligible bachelor and asked myself the question he had asked some time back. Why don't we date? I thought hard and came up with not one good answer as to why we couldn't date. I thought if he broaches the subject again, I will say 'yes'. With that resolved. I had some more fruits and went back to sleep.

I got up at 9 AM in the morning the next day and prepared a light breakfast of sandwiches. I had to maintain myself and was conscious about what I ate. I wasn't as thin as the models I worked with, but not fat either. I didn't want to put on weight and waste the lovely clothes I had in my wardrobe. Dhruva's confirmation for lunch came in the morning. 12.30 at the Taj, he had responded. I was ready for a celebratory lunch with an attractive friend. I wasn't able to think about him as just a friend after yesterday's analysis. I hoped he didn't catch it. I dressed in a chic pantsuit and went to the lunch date.

Dhruva was dressed in a pair of jeans and a light yellow shirt which suited him perfectly. He looked handsome.

He was the same age as Shradda and was successful in his chosen field, which was architecture. He was next in line to be made partner in his firm. He looked powerful. He always made it a point to arrive earlier, so that I didn't have to wait.

He looked up and saw me and gave me a salute and pulled the chair opposite him and I sat. He congratulated me and gave me a bunch of yellow roses. It was beautiful. I was happy I realised in his company. He quirked an eyebrow at me. "So quiet?" he asked. "Exhausted," I said. "It suits you," he said. "You look like a million bucks." "You look the same," I said. "Thanks for noticing." He had some questions about the show and I answered them sipping a mocktail.

He always took the initiative of ordering for both of us as per my request. The lunch date went smoothly and I thought it was time to part when he said he wanted to share some happenings with me and I agreed. We went to my house and he sat in the drawing-room and he said "Priya called me. Priya from school," he clarified. I was shocked. "Your crush?" I asked and he nodded. "She wanted to meet me as soon as possible. I wanted to ask you how you felt about that." I said, "No," boldly. He gave a half-smile.

"We have to say something to them."

"Them?"

"Shekar wants to meet you," he said.

"What is this?" I asked.

"He said they wanted to catch up." Shekar was my crush in school.

"Tell them we will meet them together. The place is your choice," I said. He agreed. "I have a meeting in 30 minutes. I will keep you updated," he said and left.

I sat in the balcony and thought of our past in Bangalore about 16 years back when I was in 11th std in a CBSE school along with Dhruva. But back then we were not such good friends. I sat with the girls and he sat with the boys. Shekar was a star in school along with Priya. They were sports champions and had many admirers and I was one of them. Dhruva as well.

Shekar was my first love and I pined for him those days. I used to sport 2 plaits and wore my uniform till my knees and was slightly introverted. If I knew someone and was secure about them, then I spoke well with them. Otherwise, I was a stone wall. No response. Shekar knew I had a crush on him, as I got tongue-tied in his presence. He used to deliberately tease me by winking at me or brushing against me. I bore it all with a smile.

Maybe he felt something for me, I thought and went dizzy from the thought. But he was a tease and so was Priya. They tortured other students who were their admirers and laughed about it with their group of friends. They announced that they had feelings for each other and I still hoped that he would look at me and feel something and break up with Priya and go out with me.

No such thing happened and I was left with a broken heart about which my hero laughed about with his friends and his girlfriend. I came to know about this because of Dhruva. He told me about these happenings as he overheard them in the canteen. I was crushed. This was humiliation and I used to think everyone was laughing at me. So I went into a shell and stayed there.

At home, there was something else brewing. My dad had discovered that my mother was having an affair with someone in the neighbourhood and he was devastated. He filed for divorce and took both me and my sister and shifted to Mumbai after getting a transfer.

This worked for me well. I decided to start afresh and got down to academics and aced my exams and then joined the best fashion technology institute in the country and came out a star student. I was picked up by a top company because of my designs and there was no looking back.

Dhruva suffered for one more year before he parted ways from that bitch. He went on to study BE architecture and joined a good company and he got back in touch with me after my third show and we became best friends from then. I had visited his house and was cordial with his parents and younger sister. Nice people. I will be damned if I let that Priya dig her talons into Dhruva. She had her chance and she blew it. Now he is my would-be boyfriend. There. I said it. That's who he was…

I drank some warm milk and went to bed. I put a reminder on my phone to call my sister tomorrow. I got up at 11 AM and took an hour for ablutions and brunch. Then I sat comfortably on my sofa and called my sister, Ramya. She wanted to know everything about the show and I obliged and in the end, I told her about Shekar and Priya.

She burst out, "How dare he, Shekar! Shradda... Please don't fall for him again."

"Nope. That is covered. I am discovering some feelings for Dhruva," I said.

"That is the best news I have heard from you for the longest time," exclaimed my sister. "Focus on him. Does he know?" she asked. "Nope," I said. "I discovered it last night." "Okay," she smiled. There was someone at the door and she had to go, so with a flurry of all the bests and take cares, we hung up.

I went through all the papers that carried our show and made some pin-ups in the draw board in my bedroom. What next Shraddha, I asked myself. Project Dhruva. She knew he will take care of her heart and not destroy it as Shekar had done. After that episode, I had shut the gates to my heart. It was platonic and I was good friends with all men that I met in the line of my work. There were some interested people and interesting people as well. But Dhruva was a perfect gentleman. I felt deep jealousy when he mentioned Priya's name. The kind that had never happened before. I knew that he had feelings for me as he had suggested dating and taking the relationship further.

This was war. Bring it on, Priya. She was no match for me, I knew. It was a gut feeling. I couldn't wait for the meeting. I felt instantly better after I had decided on my approach. I made pav bhaji and sat down to eat it. That was dinner.

The next day Dhruva called me and said they had reluctantly agreed to meet together and it was scheduled for Saturday. "Look your best, sweetheart," he said. "I plan to pull all stops."

I grinned. "So you also believe this is war?" I said. He laughed and said, "Yeah."

I worked a little bit every day from home, on the phone and online, and soon Saturday was upon me. I wore my best dress, which everyone had liked when I made it. It was a burnt orange creation and I left my hair loose after setting it. I wondered what Dhruva had worn. He looked desirable in anything he wore. The plan was that he would meet me at my house and we would go together in his car. He came on time and we looked at each other and whistled. He wore a classy shirt from Arrow complete with cuff links and a matching pair of trousers.

"So what are we to each other?" he asked with a tiny grin, which he controlled.

"Boyfriend, girlfriend," I said with resolve. He quirked his eyebrows and said, "Play act?" "Nope," I said. I meant it and looked at him worriedly. What if he had changed his mind. He grinned and said, "Then I am good. Ready to take this further?" I nodded my head and he was happy.

"Good thinking," he said. "My mother was beginning to make noises about my wedding."

I took a deep breath and said, "Sorry to keep you waiting. But not anymore."

"And instead of celebrating this, we have to meet those idiots," he grumbled.

"Oh but this is perfect," I said and kissed him on his cheek. "Let's go."

"Just for this I have a good mind to keep them waiting," he said and I peered at him to see if he was joking. He hugged me and said, 'I got over Priya on the same day you got over Shekar." I thought back to the day Dhruva had told me that Shekar was laughing at me with his friends and Priya. "You took your time getting over the hurt, but I threw it off long back. Let's go and finish this with them."

We held hands and walked to the car. They had sent a message to Dhruva confirming the time. I looked at him enquiringly. He said they were in the restaurant and waiting. I laughed. "The art of revenge by Dhruva," I said and we went slowly and reached the designated place after some 45 minutes. We went to the table where Priya and Shekar were sitting and were flabbergasted by the way they looked. Both had paunches and were dressed shabbily. Priya was in a tight shirt and jeans, which showed her bulges and Shekar was also in jeans and shirt. He was also balding. They looked bad. Dhruva and I looked at each other and forcibly keep a straight face and sat down. They looked at us agape. "Shradda and Dhruva," they parotted.

"Let's catch up," Shekar said with false humour. "Where do you work?" he asked Dhruva and Dhruva mentioned his company's name. "Wow, man! That's awesome," Shekar said.

"What's your package?"

"That's none of your business," came the reply.

"Okay, okay, okay… Peace," Shekar said. "Big shot and my slave, eh?"

"Your slave?" Dhruva erupted. "Since when, you eel?"

"Ho ho Hh… may I jog your memory. The 2 of you, you were our slaves. If only I had chosen the right college. I would have been your boss and Priya could have been a model. She is that pretty."

The waiter came to take our order. Dhruva apologised to him and said we were leaving. If those 2 wanted to order something, it was up to them. He took my hand and we left for home.

Dhruva was still fuming. He threw himself on the sofa and brooded. I went to rustle up lunch. He had a good appetite, so I cooked a proper lunch and we had it. Dhruva was silent through it. "What?" I asked. "This is not a let's get together meeting. They are up to something. I am appointing a private investigator on them. What do you think?" he asked me. I agreed.

"When do you resume work?"

"From Monday," I said.

"I will stay here till the report from the investigator comes," he said. I agreed. "On the couch," he said, his humour returning. "You said it." When I looked quizzically at him he said, "We are in a relationship." I agreed.

He called his sister and asked her to send some clothes through my driver to my residence. "Oh… anything I should know about?" she asked.

He recounted everything that had happened and she agreed with the action plan. She yelled congratulations to the 2 of us and said she would inform their parents about the situation.

I looked at Dhruva and said, "If Shekar and Priya had accepted us, then we would have been destroyed by them." "No," said Dhruva. "We would have dumped them as soon as we realised the truth."

"I hope you are right. Anyway, it's hypothetical. I am grateful for the snub, my lord," I said and did a namaste to Lord Shiva's poster in my drawing-room. Dhruva got up, hugged me and planted a kiss on my lips and said, "Do you know how long I have waited to do that?" "Around 3 years," I said and he agreed. We sat and cuddled on the sofa and I was about to ask him to rest in the spare room when the bell rang. His clothes had arrived and I showed him the room.

"You talk to the investigator and I will arrange your clothes," I said and did it. I loved the clothes he wore. Very chic! He completed his call and changed his clothes and wore a tracksuit and went to the bed. "A siesta," he said and opened his arms to me and I said, "Hold that thought," and changed. We cuddled in bed. Just as we were drifting off to sleep, the doorbell rang. He looked at me and said, "Take a wild guess."

I nodded and we went to the drawing-room and Dhruva opened the door to find Shekar and Priya at the entrance.

"Why are you here?" Priya shrieked, "This is that bitch's house."

"My girlfriend," Dhruva said and they fell silent.

"Let us in, we need to talk," said Shekar. "Nope," said Dhruva. "I don't want the 2 of you in my heaven." He asked them to leave or he would call the police.

"What are the charges?" asked Shekar.

"Trespassing," Dhruva said.

"So would you rather we went to the press with our story?" Shekar said and we looked at each other. "What story?"

"That you both were at our mercy in school. I will get a good sum of money for the scandal. That is what we wanted to negotiate with the two of you. Either accept us as your boyfriend and girlfriend or go through the scandal our story will fetch your dear girlfriend," Priya said.

I smiled at Dhruva and said, "I can handle it. I am known for my work and not for my love life."

Dhruva called the police and asked them for advice and was told that they could now be arrested for trespassing and they could unearth the plan while they spent the time in jail. He called the security and had them take them to the ground floor foyer and he went and stood there till the police came for them. He then came up to change and accompany them to the police station. I said I would accompany him and he agreed. We both wore jeans and shirts and went in Dhruva's car.

We went and filed a complaint that they were trespassing on my premises and had threatened us. This wouldn't hold them for long, Dhruva felt and he sent a message to the private investigator about what had happened. The police also will be digging into their past, I thought.

We went back home and went back to what we were doing and slept well into the night. In the morning, we woke up and had breakfast and Dhruva was about to call the police station when the investigator called and said that Shekar and Priya were married and were in the process of obtaining a divorce. No kids and failed job opportunities for both. Shekar has been asked to leave the organisation in 2 companies for fraud and Priya tried her hand at films and was now a sex worker.

They had 4 friends and they all were from school. Dhruva was able to identify them. The investigator asked if Dhruva wanted to take this to the police now and it was a resounding yes from Dhruva. He got ready and left. When I said I would join him, he said, "Not today, sweetheart. Rest for some time and I will bring lunch." I saw him off and went to his bedroom to sleep some more.

I was completely refreshed when I got up. I sat in the drawing-room, put on flute recital in the background and waited for Dhruva. He came back at 2 PM and brought North Indian thalis for both of us. We had lunch and he told me that all the 4 friends were rounded up and everyone was warned by the police and let off. The police would be keeping an eye on the gang. The arrested duo would be let off in a couple of days. Dhruva had told them that they will be let off if they gave their word that they won't go to the press and they agreed. Dhruva then didn't file an FIR. He said, "I hope that is fine with you, love," he said and I agreed.

"Even if they do go to the press, it wouldn't impact my career," I said. He agreed.

He made no mention about going back and I didn't want to mention it as well. We enjoyed each other's company. He gave strict instructions to my driver and I joined back to my office on Monday and it was a celebratory mood in the office. I was called to the partner's cabin and he thanked me for my impeccable work and said, "A big project is headed our way because of our show's success."

It was a collaboration with a Paris fashion house and he wanted to know if I would be interested in participating. I grabbed the opportunity and said, "Of course." He said the details would be sent to us for our opinion and he would call for a conference with all the people who had agreed to be part of this project. I thanked him for the opportunity and left his cabin.

I thought of calling Dhruva and decided I will. He is my boyfriend and I have every right to call him at work and disturb him, I thought and called him. He answered on the second ring. "Are you busy?" I asked him. He said yes and I said, "Good, I am disturbing you." He laughed and said that was fine and he would catch up. I then revealed the reason for my excitement and he was happy about my growth. "Congrats! I will book a table for dinner tonight. Just the 2 of us."

I said, "That's a splendid idea," and hung up. I felt buoyed by his presence and extremely happy. The day passed on in a positive atmosphere and I decided to draw some sketches for the project and had a handful by the end of the day. I put it in my locker and left for home sweet home. He was home before me and was working on something on his laptop. He closed it as soon as I came home and hugged me and planted a kiss on my lips. "That's it?" I asked him with raised eyebrows. He said, "The rest after marriage," with a smile.

I went into his arms and hugged him. "How do you know that I won't be comfortable with an affair before marriage?" I asked him. "You mentioned it about 3 years back, I feel the same," he said. I recalled the conversation. "Let's get ready for dinner. We have half an hour." I scooted to my room and he went to his room.

It was the most romantic dinner. The table was next to the pool and it was candlelit. There was a bouquet of red roses on the table, which Dhruva gave to me. There was music in the background and my boyfriend looked like a Greek god. There was champagne. The entire evening was intoxicating. I told him, I could get used to this treatment. Dhruva answered, "Me too," and was looking at me. He asked for a dance and we swayed to the music for a while and sat down to eat. It was Italian cuisine.

There was music in my heart as we went home to my apartment and I went to his room after changing and lay down with him. He grabbed me and cuddled and I got up to leave. He said, "After marriage," and I answered in the affirmative and went to my room to sleep.

The next day was bright and sunny and a wonderful start as Dhruva came with a breakfast tray to my bed and climbed in next to me. We had sandwiches and coffee and got ready for work. "I could get used to this," I said and planted a kiss on his lips. "Good," he said. "This is forever for me," he said. "Me too," I said. "I have waited enough. I am going to talk to your sister soon," he said. I agreed and cursed myself for all the time I had wasted.

"We have to think about our family as well and I want kids. 2 of them," he said. "Me too," I said. "I will have a talk with my parents today," he said. But before that, he went down on his knees and proposed. I said it was purely my good fortune and extended my left hand and he slid in the ring. It was a platinum ring with diamonds on it. "This is the engagement ring," he said and I felt euphoric.

Everyone noticed the ring at work and I told them I was engaged. Dhruva, on the other hand, told everyone who looked at him that he was engaged, he told me when I called to disturb him. I got a call from his mother and I was slightly nervous, but she dispelled the nervousness by telling me that I made Dhruva happy and that was all they wanted as parents. She said she was proud that I was going to be her daughter-in-law because of my career graph as well. I thanked her and asked if she wanted to see my office. She exclaimed, "Yes, please."

"I will arrange for it as soon as possible, Mom," I said. She blessed me and hung up.

I mentioned it to Dhruva. "Why didn't you tell me she would like to visit my office?" I asked him. "If I knew about it, I would have done it," he said. "I will bring her tomorrow. I want her to see the insides as well. I will get permission," I said. "You and Mom." He was okay with the idea.

I went to Dhruva's house that evening and met his family. I asked Mom, "Do you design?" She said, "Yes. How did you guess?" Dhruva and his sister, Meghna were surprised. Apparently, only Dad, who goes by the name

Prashant knew about it. "Mom, do you want to show it to me?" She looked at her husband and said, "Moment of truth," and got up to bring her folder to me. "The truth dear," she said. "Yes mama," I said and I went through the designs. There was a steep learning curve from the first design to the last. "How many years, Mama? This seems a lot," asked Dhruva. "About 3 years," she said and smiled at me.

"Your last design would have gotten you a job in a fashion house," I said and hugged her. "What do you want to do, Mom?" I asked her. "You can work as a freelancer or get a job like mine in a fashion house. Or you can open a boutique of your own. Your business," I said.

"I want to work as a freelancer for a short period and then open my own business," she said and asked her husband if it was possible,money-wise. He said, "My money is intact. Dhruva doesn't let us spend a single paisa. Whatever you want to do."

Dhruva said, "Mom, I will invest in your business." I said, "Me too, Mom."

"Mom I want to work in your boutique with you," Meghana said. "Sumithra's designs," Dhruva said. Dhruva asked Shradda to give the names of fashion houses and said he would send the designs. I said okay and gave him the list.

"I have got permission for you to see my work premises tomorrow. Can you make it?" I asked Dhruva. He said, "Yes. I am relatively free in the morning."

"Then make it at 10.30. You, Mom?" I asked Mom. She said she couldn't wait.

Mom then said, "Now, let's discuss your nupitals." "Okay," we all said. "Give us your sister's phone number. We will talk to her."

Dhruva sent it to them. "She is updated," he said and laughed at my expression.

"She was firmly in my corner," he said. "And we keep in touch." I was happy. He said the engagement was over. "Half over," I said and took out a ring box from my bag and asked for his hand. He extended his left hand and I inserted the ring I had bought. It was a replica of my ring without the diamonds.

I could see that his family were very happy. Meghana took a video and sent it to my sister, Ramya and her husband Vivek. "Now, leave the rest to us. We will plan it. I have designed a gagra choli for the wedding. Would you like to see it?" Sumithra asked me. I had tears in my eyes. "Yes, Mama," I said and she brought the designs. A shervani for Dhruva and a gagra for me. They were exquisite. "Thank you, Mom," I said. She hugged me.

"I wasn't sure if you would wear it."

"It's the most beautiful dress I have ever seen," I said. "Likewise, Mom," Dhruva said. "What about for Dad and Meghana and yourself?" Dhruva asked. "Shradda's designs," Mom said and I laughed. "Give me 2 days, I will design it," I said. Dhruva then said he wanted to stay at my place till the wedding. His parents agreed and I vigorously nodded my head. "Platonic, Mom and Dad," we said in unison. They smiled and said, "Good."

I took Dhruva and Sumithra around my office and the workshop, which was attached to the office building the next day. Mom almost wept. But it was apparent to everyone who interacted with her that this was a dream come true for her. I looked at Dhruva and he nodded. I left 2 of her designs with the partner's secretary. Mom spent more time in the workshop, looking at the machines and she said, "I need help with these machines when I set up my business," and looked at me. "I will do it, Mama," I said. "No worries. In fact last night I had done the math and it is with Dhruva now." Dhruva smiled at her. "We will show it to you at lunch." She wiped her tears away.

We went for lunch to Mom's favourite restaurant and Dhruva and I explained the machines and the amount that we needed to raise for the boutique. She looked at it keenly and added 2 more machines that she had seen in the workshop and rounded the figures. I received a call from my office and my partner said he liked both the designs and asked me whose it was. I said, "My mother in law to-be. She wanted to do a little freelancing before opening her boutique."

My partner said he wanted 2 more designs along the same lines and he was hiring her. I said, "She is here if you want to talk to her."

"Of course," he said and I passed the phone to Sumithra. She was nervous. Dhruva held her hand and encouraged her. She spoke impeccably and agreed to his terms and she, in turn, said he could not pin her to the timelines and when she decided, she would leave the job for her own boutique. He appeared to have agreed. He asked her to come to the office the next day to sign the contract. She said she would bring her husband and he agreed.

Dhruva ordered gulab jamoon with rabdi for everyone. I then asked Arun to drop Mama home and then come back. Dhruva and I left for work after seeing Sumithra off.

The rest of the day went smoothly. I left early as I had finished my work at home. My designs were approved by my partner and so I was relaxed. I reached home and got down to preparing a 3-course meal. North Indian, Dhruva's favourite. I was done in an hour and a half. I then dressed for dinner. He came home and whistled slowly at the spread on the table. He saw me and whistled again. "This is heaven," he said. "Except for me. I will change in a jiffy. Meet you at the dining table sweetheart," he said and went to his room.

I was pleased with his reaction and smiled. When he joined me at the table, we were just about to start on our food, when the doorbell rang. He said he would open it. I watched from the drawing-room. It was my mother. "Shraddha, can you come here, love," he called and I went to join him at the entrance. It was most definitely my mother. "She is saying…" he said and I interrupted and said, "My mother."

He let her into the drawing-room and asked her why she was here. She laughed and said, "My house, you stupid man. My daughter." This was the first time I was meeting her after the divorce. Apparently, she kept tabs on us. I just stood and watched her. Dhruva's arm was around me. "What do you want?" I asked her and she responded, "To stay here with you. He has to go. He is not your husband and so he cannot stay here. We are Indians after all. No premarital affair and no extramarital affairs. That's what your dad would have said," she exclaimed.

"What I do is none of your business," I said. "I want to stay with you in my twilight years." "Twilight? I bet you have your claws in another man. You cannot stay here," I said. "I go out in the morning and come at night. Why can't I stay the nights here with my daughter," she said. "Vatsala, you can stay the night but I will bolt the door from outside," said Dhruva.

I gave him a surprised look and he just looked at me and I agreed with him. He has a plan, I thought. She agreed after thinking about it for a little while. "Okay, then sit," he said and got her a plate of the food I had prepared.

"I will come to the dining table," she said and we both said, "No." He then carried me to the table and sat next to me and fed me with his hands. I did the same after I got my emotions under control. Tears started falling as I recounted what a wonderful mother and woman Sumithra was. He carried me to my room and laid me gently on the bed and sat till I was calm. Then he left to see what Vatsala was doing.

She was going through my cupboards and checking everything in the dining room and drawing room area. Dhruva said she could retire to the bedroom. He bolted her in and came back to me. "I think maybe she has planted a device or two in the house," he said. "I will take tomorrow off and debug the house with an expert. I will install a CCTV camera in the drawing room. Hidden," he said and looked at me. "Is that okay?" I nodded my head.

"We will leave as usual and I will come back with the specialists. I will keep you posted," he said and I agreed. "I think I will tap the landline," he said. "Whatever you want to do, Dhruva," I said. He sat by my side till I dropped off to sleep and then went to his room.

The next day things went as per plan and I got a thumbs-up message from Dhruva at around noon. I responded 'I love you'. He replied, 'Now. When I am stuck in office'. I send a heart emoji and he did the same. 'Your timing sucks,' he said and I laughed.

I had a conference meeting with our collaborators from Paris and I went with good humour and it was a good meet with my designs being approved by everybody. I left the meeting and asked Dhruva if I could go early home as I had to work for another client. He said I could. He would bring work home as well in that case. He had to present a design to his clients as well. So I left with the designs I had sent them last to modify some and to redesign some. I changed into tracks and sat in the drawing-room on the floor and started work.

Dhruva came soon after. He also sat on the floor and it was so good sitting and working together. I said, "We will ask Mom to work with us as well after marriage." He agreed. He got news from Sumithra that she had signed a contract for freelancing. We were ecstatic. Dad sent sweets to us. It was 1kg of badam halwa. I squealed in delight. Dhruva sent a thank you from both of us. We dug in. Dad said Sumithra wanted to work with us. I sent a welcome to our home to all the 3 of them. "I will prepare dinner," I said.

They said they would come in 30 minutes. I was at my culinary best. No dessert, as we had badam halwa. Dhruva came and tasted everything at regular intervals. He called it helping. I was amused.

"And? How is it?"

"It is the best food I have had," he declared. I wish Ramya was also here.

"Maybe soon, you can never say," he said.

Soon everybody came and we had early dinner and they gave me a 5-star rating. Then we all sat down to work. I loved every bit of it. I felt warm and loved to be a part of a great family. Sumithra sat next to me and proclaimed that she was sitting next to her idol. "Mommy, I shrieked and hugged her. I showed her all my designs. She asked me what I do with unapproved designs.

"I try to make something else with it. But I discard the originals."

"I want them," Mom said.

"Mom, I will give you good ones, I said. "No dear, I want this." She showed me my discarded designs. I handed it over to her. "All yours, Mom," I said. Dad asked her, "You plan to change it."

"Yes.very slightly. For my boutique."

I went to my room and came back with the discarded file and handed it to her. "Thank you, my dear. Now I cannot fail."

"You won't," we chorused. She then sat down to draw her designs. I gave her my spare sketch pen and crayons. Dad sat next to her and tried to help. It was cute to watch. I had a permanent smile on my face. Tea was supplied by Meghana. I soon completed my work and sat with Sumithra. Mom took a deep breath and I went on to check her designs. It was fantastic work and I suggested some changes for practicality and she and dad agreed.

"Anyone for some pakodas," I asked? All hands went up. Meghana came to me slightly upset. Dhruva looked at her and at me. I nodded and went to the kitchen. "Bhabhi, what about me?" she asked. She had completed her degree in finance. I said, "You will be the CFO of the boutique. Let's find a CA and you can take instructions from her or him."

She immediately brightened. "Dhruva and I will help." My family heard it and Dad said, "I thought that was fixed, child," he said. She beamed.

I gave her the costing Dhruva and I had done and asked her to call the businesses that were selling the machines we wanted and to check the prices with them. She took a keen look at the costing and took another paper and started working. I made onion pakodas and we all had our fill.

They all left at 10 PM. Mom said, "Next time we will do this at our house. I am going to focus on my work. So we need a cook soon." Dad smiled and said, "It will be done." They left in Dad's car.

"Is there anything left from the dinner?" Dhruva asked sheepishly. I said, "Nope love." He smiled. He made some sandwiches. "It's time." Vatsala had said she would return home at 8 PM. We watched some TV and waited. She came at around 10.30 PM and said she was ready for dinner. Dhruva handed her the sandwiches and said, "Eat and go to your room." She ate enroute to her room. She saw some of Shradda's designs in the drawing-room and grabbed it and came back to the drawing-room, where we were seated and threatened to set the designs on fire if she didn't get what she wanted. She wanted cash and jewellery. "Now," she exclaimed.

When we didn't react, she got out a lighter from her blouse and lit it. It caught flame and fell on the ground. The doorbell rang just then and we saw that Shekar and Priya were again in the entrance. Dhruva called the police and informed them about what had happened. They said they will be at our house ASAP. "But how will you prove that she did it?" Shekar asked. "It's your word against ours."

That's when we knew that Vatsala was with them. For money. "If you don't do as we say, we will keep popping up in your lives. Money, jewellery and marriages with us and a home for your mother," said Priya. "Do you want to negotiate?"

We both shook our heads and said, "No." The police would talk to them. "Without evidence what can you possibly do to us?" Shekar asked. We didn't utter a word. He then went on to explain their modus operandi and what they did and the success they had over the years and how they escaped the law as they didn't leave evidence. By then, the police had arrived and arrested them. Dhruva gave them a copy of the footage. Dhruva had messaged the police to come after an hour. They were listening to the confessions and then came for the arrest.

All the 3 had done enough to remain in jail for a long time. "And after we come out? What then?" Shekar asked Dhruva. "I can protect my family. That is a given," Dhruva said. "If you know what's good for you, you will stay away." "They are not coming out," the police inspector said. They had on camera that they had attempted to kill at least a couple of their victims. I had missed it in the confessional.

"So that's that," Dhruva concluded and they left. Dhruva went with them to the police station along with me and he called Dad and ask him to come to the police station directly. Dad was waiting there when we arrived there and we filed an FIR and signed. Dad hugged me and said, "That's it, child. Now only happiness." I said, "Can't wait, Dad." We then left for home.

Dhruva instructed me to go to sleep and said he would follow suit. I agreed and went to my room and thought about the day's happenings. He was checking when they could disconnect the CCTV cameras. He was instructed by the police to hire a good lawyer. He knew 2 lawyers and asked them who would be adept at this case. He got a name and phone number and left it for tomorrow. When he came to my room to check on me, I said, "Let's keep the CCTV." And he nodded. I was thinking the same thing. We hugged and kissed and he went to his room to lay it down on paper to show to the lawyer.

The next morning Dhruva was at work at home and I had to go to meet the collaborators. He waved me off after a kiss and I went to work in a happy frame of mind. I thought I would check with one of the partners about my discarded designs. I was told I could not sell them as all of my designs belonged to the business house. But if I planned to open a boutique and quit my job, then it belonged to me. I had to make some changes to the designs. I made up my mind and thanked him.

I discussed it with Dhruva that evening and he was shocked. "But what about your career?" "This is my career. Do you mind?" I asked. "Hell NO!" he said. "I want you to think this through," he said. "I have," I said. "I will quit after the Paris show, which is in a week. I don't get to go there, you know. The partners will go. Now it is time to take the next step. Of course, Mom should agree," I said. "Let's go and meet them," he said.

We went to his place and I gave mom an application for a job and asked her approval. She jumped up and yelled "Shraddha!" Dad looked at us for an explanation. Dhruva plucked the letter from his mom's grip and gave it to dad. He was shocked. "But my dear child you have your own label." "Yes. And this is the next step," I said. "But Mom didn't answer," I said worriedly.

She pulled me up and hugged me. "Yes," she said. "It will be called Shraddha's." "Nope," I said. "Shraddha's and Sumithra's." "This is huge," Dad told Dhruva. He agreed.

"Now we need to call a bank and do this as per Shradda's clout," Dad told mom.

"Dad, we will just go with Mom's plans. I will slide in," I said.

"Nope."

Dhruva and Prashant shook their heads. "Let's meet after Ramya and Vivek move to Mumbai."

"They are moving to Mumbai?" I asked Dhruva, and he replied in the affirmative. Now my family was complete.

"You will quit and then relax for at least 2 months," Mom said. "And we will have a wedding then. We will open the boutique after the wedding and see where it takes us."

"Places," Dhruva said and Mom smiled.

"Now she is not scared," Prashant declared and Mom smiled and said, "Yes."

Epilogue

The wedding was a beautiful event and Shraddha moved into Dhruva's house. Ramya and her family moved into Shraddha's place on rent

The boutique took off as soon as it was opened and the entire family including Ramya and Vivek were involved. It was a family affair.

Coming of Age

I was in a happy state of mind as I watched the rain fall from my balcony in my apartment in Mumbai. My theatre rehearsals went well yesterday in the evening and it was Sunday. I had a special bonding with Sundays. I checked the clock and it said 5 PM. I decided to make some pakodas for myself. I had learnt the art of cooking the hard way. A lot of trial and error and following recipes downloaded from the web. So I was proud of the skill.

I had some onions and I made the pakoda mix and added onions to it and deep-fried them and it came out very tasty. I sat down to eat it. Initially, I was not too inclined towards cooking at home as it was difficult to cook for one, and I stayed alone in my 2 bedroom apartment, which my dad had left me. God bless his soul I thought.

He had passed on 4 years back and my mom and I lived in the apartment. But as we got estranged, my mom left the house and stayed with some friends of hers and was now living with her boyfriend in his pad. I was grateful to my dad for this inheritance and he had also left 20 lakhs for me. I kept it in a fixed deposit for a rainy day. I was an actress and worked in theatre. I attended workshops and had a small group of friends with whom I hung out. We met almost every day as we were sometimes in the same play. Income from this passion of mine was not that great, but I was able to sustain myself. I thought, maybe I should get a day job like some have done and keep this as a hobby. It is about time, I thought. I should start thinking about my future as well.

As I was thinking about it the landline rang and it was my mom, Sonal. She called to check if I was doing okay and if I needed something. "Not from you," I said and took a deep breath. "I am okay, Mom," I said and asked, "Can I hang up?"

She sighed and said, "Okay, Tara," and I hung up. My mom and I shared an uneasy relationship from the beginning. She was a star in the world of theatre and I got the acting bug from her. But that was all I shared with her. She was an extrovert and she and dad shared a volatile relationship. They couldn't live with each other and they couldn't live without each other, my dad had once said. My dad died of a brain tumour and I blamed her for his death and also there was the fact that she moved on pretty soon. She started dating and started a relationship with a man 5 years her junior. Mihir was 45 to her 50 and they started living together and it had been 4 years.

Sonal tried to explain things from her point of view, but I rejected it and left the room. She called every Sunday to talk to me and I rejected her olive branch. I picked up my book, which was the play that we were going to release next week and immersed myself in it. I wanted a career like my mom's. Let's see where this takes me, I thought and went to sleep after finishing off the pakodas.

We had rehearsals every day for 1 hour in the evening till the play opened and after that the show was for 1 hour in the evening. So I was totally free in the morning. I thought about a second career the next day and was going through the internet for options. I was a graduate in the arts and I wanted something exciting. Not the usual office from 9 AM to 5 PM. I thought about becoming an RJ in one of the radio stations.

I had a fair knowledge of Hindi songs and movies as I was an avid Bollywood follower. So I rang them up one by one to check if they could employ me. 3 of them turned me down and 1 said they would like to meet me and take a voice audition. I agreed and I was told to go to their office at 11 AM.

I got ready and went to see them. Hindi was my mother tongue and I thought I aced the test, but they kept me in suspense and said they would reach out to me if the manager liked my tape. I went back to my house and put my mind to my play again. I was thinking about the nuances and the feel of my character. It was not the lead. I was a character in the play and I was yet to scale the heights to reach the lead part. I thought that maybe I should take tips from my mother but then rejected the idea.

I left for my rehearsals in the evening. No call from the radio station so far. It was a powerful play and I was happy to be a part of it. It was against corruption and was written beautifully. The writer Sudhanshu was the director as well. He wasn't the jolly type. Quite the opposite in fact and intense. He was a perfectionist. I was learning a lot under his tutelage.

Today, the rehearsals went well. He was happy. He asked me to stay back after as he wanted to talk to me about my character. So I stayed back in the evening. It was 8 PM and it had started raining. After everyone had left, he sat with me and explained the character to the minutest detail. I listened with rapt attention. Once he was through, which was about 40 minutes later, it had started to rain even more heavily. He asked me where I stayed and said he had to pass it to go to his address and so he would drop me in his second-hand car. I agreed.

He drove slowly as the rain had become a deluge and there was no scope for conversation. We reached my house after about an hour and I asked him if he wanted some tea before he went to his house. He agreed, to my surprise. As we were having tea, he asked me about myself and I told him about my lineage. He was surprised and asked me if my mother helped me with the characters I played. I told him the truth. "That's sad," he said.

He didn't say anything about her as he noticed that my mood changed when we discussed her. He told me about his life. He had a father who lived in Kolkata and they hadn't met in a while because of their busy schedules. His mother had passed away last year and his dad lived in a joint family so he had someone to look after him. He said, "I was in the IT industry and theatre was a hobby. But after about 10 years in it, I decided to pursue theatre as my main career. I am a fulltime theatre writer and director now."

I said I had applied for the job of an RJ and had given audition but had not got a response from them. He said that was a good career option. He left soon after and the rain had become a drizzle. I cooked a couple of rotis and had them with curd. I had to maintain myself. So I had rotis in the night for dinner. I avoided rice as much as possible.

He called the next morning as I was going through my piece again and asked if I would like to go to the beach with him. I agreed readily. It was my favourite spot. We sat near the shore and watched the waves for some time. Then we had some chat which was being offered there. I got a call on my mobile and it was from the radio station. They asked if I was open to the morning slot from 7 to 8 AM and I said I was.

I was an early riser and early to bed at night. So I had no issues about the timings. I bagged the job. It felt fantastic. I shared the news with Sudhanshu and he was encouraging. "You are still young. You should not stick to only theatre. You should experience other careers as well," he said. I had to join from tomorrow and I had to leave early as well. I asked him about his age. He said he was 35 years old. That was 11 years my senior. I told him my age and said, "I will do this for 10 years just like you. I could use the money."

We had pav Bhaji for lunch and then headed home. He dropped me home and said he would pick me up and drop me every day as he had to pass my house to get to his house. I agreed as it was a big help for me. Especially because of the rain in the evening. He came to pick me up in the evening and we went for the rehearsals. He told me about the characters he had written in his plays and I was a rapt listener. I absorbed it and my performance in the evening was my best as per my colleagues and friends opinion. Sudhanshu said the same. I said, "Thanks to your mentoring."

The show opened with fantastic performances and applause from the audience. It was a runaway hit. Our performances were received well from the critics as well. I kept the clippings and thanked my mentor profusely. This was the first time, I got such good reviews and I was ecstatic. My mom called me on Sunday to congratulate me and I thanked her and then hung up. Sudhanshu watched it with a blank expression. He didn't comment on it and I was grateful for the reprieve.

The show was house full for 3 months and we took a break after that. My day job with the radio station was proceeding as per plan. I couldn't be happier I told my friends.

"I think you could be," Sudhashu said and I asked him how.

He said, "All in good time. I have to prepare for my next production. It is a new play. Would you be interested in playing a part?" I said, "Yes, please," and he laughed. "Are you sure? I wouldn't allow you to withdraw later once you learn about the cast and the story," he said and I said I would not. "Okay," he said.

After the play ended, we had a party to celebrate the success and we were in high spirits after it. "The play will revert after a break," Sudhanshu told the newspapers.

He had given the selected artists the news about the next play. "The rehearsals are in the same place," he said. He handed the script to the selected actors and we were told to report for the rehearsals the next day. I was looking forward to reading it. I got the time the next day after my RJ stint. It was about a strained relationship between a successful mother and her daughter. I was zapped. The part was tailor-made for me and my mother. Realisation dawned on me. The lead would be my mother, that's why Sudhanshu had said I shouldn't withdraw from the play.

I sat with my head in my hands and took a deep breath. Professionally, this was a dream part with an established actress. It meant I was catching the eye of the producers and writers and If this was successful, then I would have arrived in the theatre world. I would be in her orbit again and she would try to bridge the gap. I told myself I will have to detach and I cannot afford to miss this opportunity. I made a pact with myself and got ready to read the script once again as a character of the daughter. Just then Mom called on the landline and I thought it was best to talk to her with detachment.

I picked the receiver and said, "Yes, Mom." She sounded happy. She said, "I called to check if I can accept the part in the new play written by Sudhanshu. I will accept it if you are okay with it. He told me that you have agreed to do the daughter part." That was decent, I thought and I said, "Up to you, Mom. I will do it. It's a breakthrough for me."

"Agreed, dear," she said. "I will agree to it as I want to spend some time with you." I didn't respond to that. But that didn't deter her. She sounded happy when she hung up. She said, "See you this evening, dear," and she hung up.

In the evening after everyone showed up, the rehearsals started and my mom, as usual, took center stage and made a powerful impact in the first scene. I felt pale in comparison and so did Sudhanshu. Sonal suggested some changes to me for my part and I snapped at her.

"Are you the writer?" I asked sarcastically. She replied, "No, dear. Just a suggestion," and there were tears in her eyes. Everyone was flabbergasted at my response to a helpful superstar. I stormed off the stage and sat alone in the theatre hall. Sudhanshu looked furious at me and I wilted. "Damn it," I said under my breath. "Just when everything was falling into place." I went and apologised to Sudhanshu. He just stared at me. I walked to the stage and went through the rest of my play and sat alone waiting for the group around Sudhanshu to disperse.

He sat with my mother and asked her for sometime tomorrow morning at a place of her choice. He said, "I need to discuss something with you." She said, "Come to my house, dear. I will send you the address." He agreed. She said, "Tara is waiting for you," and patted his cheek. "I will see you tomorrow."

"How will you go?" Sudhanshu asked. "My ride is here," she said and pointed towards a handsome man sitting in the end row. "That's my love. He didn't want to intrude on Tara," she said. "I will see you tomorrow," she said and went towards Mihir.

That evening Sudhanshu was silent and I deduced he must still be angry with me. I was silent as well. He dropped me off and said, "See you tomorrow," and left. I was hurting in the chest area which was filled with emotions. I went home and tried to sleep but tears came instead. I wept well into the night and made a resolution that I would be professional with Sonal. I have to think of her as Sonal, I told myself. That night I grew up just a little. A change came over me and I felt it.

I breezed through the RJ job the next morning and spent the rest of the time immersing myself in the character of my play. In the evening, I was more equipped to handle my situation. I behaved cordially with everyone and I told Sonal about my decision. She agreed," Whatever you want, beta," she said and she gave some suggestions as well on how to play my character and I thanked her and tried it.

It worked and I could feel it myself and everyone noticed it and they all wanted suggestions from Sonal. She was the centre of attention everywhere she went. Nothing has changed, I noted. She wore cotton sarees and had a big bindi on her forehead and wore wooden bangles and she attracted people like a magnet. I was the complete opposite. I did my job and went and sat by myself. The performances were very good. Sudhanshu looked happy today. He came to me and said, "I will need 20 minutes please," and I nodded my head, happy that he was speaking to me again.

He was making small changes to the script and that's why he needed time, I deduced. "No change for you," he said. "You just need to put it a little more emotion, that's all," he said and asked me if I was ready to leave. I looked at Sonal and she waved at the man in the balcony and he said he was coming down. Mihir, I thought. "Tara, my child, see you tomorrow," she said loudly and there was a gasp from my colleagues who were present there. "She is your daughter?" someone exclaimed. "Yes," replied Sonal. "And I am a proud mama," she said and went towards the entrance. Sudhanshu came to me and took my arm and we left as dramatically.

After he dropped me at the entrance of my house, Sudhanshu said, "If you want to talk about your relationship with your parents, I am always available. Just give me a call, and I smiled at him and said I will tell him when.

The next day, after my stint at the radio station, I sat and went through the script and put my real emotions when

I dealt with my mom into the role. I decided I will use the emotions that I feel when I encounter her. The rehearsals were a tremendous success. Mom understood the emotions that I displayed and tried to explain it in the course of the play. I wasn't in the mood to listen to her. I let it slide and went to my place alone in the theatre. Mom was happy and she spent her time talking to everyone and Sudhanshu. He came and sat with me and said he would be happy if I joined others. I smiled at him and said, "From tomorrow."

Whenever I saw him looking at my acting and happy, I felt buoyed and happy myself. He was my anchor in this turbulent time in my life. We went home and I felt drained because of the emotions that I experienced in the rehearsals, so I drank some milk and crashed in my bed.

Sudhanshu called the next day and asked, "Beach?" I was relieved that my relationship with him hadn't been impacted because of my relationship with my mother and said, "Yes." We went to the beach and sat and watched the waves and I said, "My mom used to bring me here when I was a kid and I fell in love with the soothing effect the waves had on me. I am a frequent visitor to the beach. I wish I had spent more time with her then. But she was always busy and my dad was busy in his own world of drinks, friends and affairs."

"You knew about it then?" he asked. "Not initially," I responded. "But as I grew older, Mom's fights with him grew and I heard it and put it together. Mom was the breadwinner and he may have abused her physically, she never told me anything, so I don't know for sure. Now she is ready to talk and I am feeling saturated. I don't want to go to the past'. That's my story."

"Did he raise his hand to you?" Sudhanshu asked.

"Yes, once."

"I see," he said.

"Why didn't you tell your mom about that?"

"I hardly saw her those days. She was busy with her work. It was a lonely childhood," I said. Sudhanshu hugged me and asked, "What about now?"

'No," I said. "You and my friends are there and I feel happy whenever I spend time with you and them. He looked happy. "Good," he said.'I am always here for you. Don't forget that," he said and I felt the happiness inside me grow.

That evening, at the rehearsals, I didn't feel the emotion that always clogged my throat when I meet Mom, and the ache in the heart also had disappeared. For the first time, I felt free of all the negativity that surrounded me about my mother. I was thankful to Sudhanshu for listening to me in the afternoon. Needless to say, my performance was exemplary. Mom was impressed, so was Sudhanshu. I would arrive in the theatre world with this play. I knew it in my bones. I sat with everyone and they spoke to me about the metamorphosis and Mom took the stage to explain the tricks of the trade and I watched her and felt good about myself.

I saw Mihir sitting in the last row and Mom waving at him when she wanted to leave. There were tears in her eyes. She asked me, "Would it be inappropriate to hug you? You have grown up in a week in front of my eyes."

I said, "Not now, Mom." She accepted it and left. Sudhanshu stood up and hugged me and said he was extremely proud of me. I was in seventh heaven and he noticed it and gave me a lopsided grin. The mood in the car was different and both Sudhanshu and I noticed it. I smiled at him and got down at my apartment. I grew up a little more that day and I was filled with positivity.

I could feel all eyes on me the next morning at the radio station. My colleague asked, "Did something happen yesterday? Did you fall in love?"

I said, "I fell in love with myself."

"Suits you," he said and smiled at me. Now I didn't cringe when people mentioned my mother's name. The radio station had requested for a conversation with my mom about the play and I volunteered to take the request to her and they were happy about that. It was at 11 AM and someone else would do the interview.

That day after the rehearsals, I took my manager's request to her and her face bloomed. "Of course, yes," she said. "Will you do the interview?" she asked and I shook my head.

"One of my colleagues. It's at 11 AM."

"I will do it," she said.

I said, "Someone from the station will get in touch with you about this." I turned around and said, "Thank you, Mom." She wept silently. I wanted to know why but I didn't ask. I thought Sudhanshu would know. Maybe I will ask him, I thought. Maybe. There was a smile on my lips these days because of him.

That evening while going home, I asked Sushandhu, "Do you know why Mom was crying today after the rehearsals?" He smiled and said, "No, why didn't you ask her?"

"I don't want her to think I care about her."

"Oh, does that mean you don't care about her?"

"Yes," I said. "I am going through my life in the best way possible, I don't want any more complications."

"Okay," Sudhanshu said and I looked at him keenly. He appeared honest. "How did you think my rehearsals went today?" And I became immersed in his explanations.

The next day Mom cried more. I asked her why against my better judgement. She said, "When you are ready to hear my point of view, I will tell you."

I said, "That day may not come."

She said, "I have faith in my goddess Durga. She will make it happen."

I left her to sit with my friends. They were appreciative of my performance and wanted some tips based on what I had done. I obliged. The show opened with packed theatres. Mom's conversation on the radio station helped. Sudhanshu said and it was a super hit.

"We have to get ready for a longer duration for this play," Sudhanshu told us and we were only too happy to do it. The normal duration was 3 months with Sudhanshu. He then took a break. But this was a play that was critically acclaimed and had mass appeal because of Mom. The next day's newspaper had the headlines 'The tigress and her cub'. I was flattered. The article had an analysis of my performance and my mom's. I was right in thinking this would be my breakthrough play and I was proved right. I got some offers in television and Mom got offers for movies. She said she would take it up only after the show took a break as theatre was her first love. I felt the same.

Sudhanshu went around in a good mood and a ready smile. He was offered to direct a movie and write the script and he was enthused about it. He told me, "I will start on the script. They have given me a free hand. How about working in a movie?" I laughed and said, "I hadn't thought about it. It's time you and your mom did."

We had a success party sponsored by Sudhanshu and Mom came resplendent in a printed silk with Mihir and I went in a cotton saree and a sleeveless blouse. Mom brought Mihir to me and introduced him as her partner. I said a polite 'hello' and moved away from them. I could see the tears forming in Mom's eyes and said, "You have to stop doing that."

She said it was 'involuntary. Mihir hugged her and asked if she wanted to leave. "No," she said. "I want to stay back and watch her." I left them and went to my group. Sudhanshu had ordered a momento for all the actors and we were presented them among fanfare and laughter. I was extremely happy.

That night I invited Sudhanshu to my apartment after he had dropped me and he said, "It would not be just coffee and you are not ready for that. I will wait. I smiled at him shyly and said, "Good night," and went to my house. I was thinking about my next step career-wise. Why not a movie? I asked myself. Sudhanshu is directing, so there would not be any exploitation and it would improve my resume. I decided to ask him about the part tomorrow. I slept blissfully. My earnings were looking good with the 2 jobs and I had started saving as well. I was in a happy space.

The next day when Sudhanshu picked me up, I posed the question to him. He smiled and said, "Tempted?" I nodded. "Only because you will be directing."

"I will let you know. I am thinking of you as a parallel lead."

I said, "I cannot wait to hear the script."

He looked happy. "Let's see what your mother says," he said. "Her first question was, is Tara doing it?" I smiled but did not comment. "Now I will tell her Tara might do it."

"No. Tara will do it," I said.

"Okay," he said and we went to our destination and the show started amidst applause.

Sonal came after the play ended and asked me, "Doing Sudhanshu's movie?"

I said, "Yes, Mom." She asked me, "Do you mind if I take it up?"

"I want to spend time with you," she said. I said, "Do what you want, Mom."

She smiled and left. Sudhanshu had 2 actors in the bag, I thought. But a movie is a different ball game altogether and I asked Sudhanshu, "Will you conduct a workshop for us? We are theatre actors and I don't know how to act in a movie."

He said, "I will arrange it."

The play was running to packed houses and Sudhanshu got a request to stage the play for 1 week in Delhi and Kolkata. He was ecstatic as he would get to meet his father in Kolkata. He asked all of us if we wanted to go and we agreed unanimously. I haven't been out of Mumbai and I was looking forward to the trips. Mom said she wanted to bring her partner and Sudhanshu said, "Of course, you can. All of you can bring whoever you want to. But you will have to pay for your kin."

First, we went to Delhi and we roamed around the place and I went shopping along with Sudhanshu. Mom tagged along with Mihir. She picked a gorgeous saree and then some salwar suits. I picked some long skirts and salwar suits. Sudhanshu was upset that I hadn't picked sarees. He bought one for me and I promised to wear it whenever he said. Mom alternated between tears and happiness. It was a good outing, I thought. I got some stoles for my friends at the radio station.

"I will take you for the best shopping of your life in Kolkata," Sudhanshu told me.

"We will come along," Mihir said. Sudhanshu looked at me questioningly. I said I had no objections.

The play was a stupendous success and so was the trip. We went to Kolkata from there for a week and our work was appreciated by the critics there and the shows were house full. Sudhanshu, as promised, took me, Mom and Mihir to the shopping hot spots.

"Oh, but you should have told me," I wailed. "I would have picked less in Delhi. These are gorgeous. I wanted to save some money, but it will have to wait. I will not shop in Mumbai for a while. The prices are very good as well."

I picked up a lehenga and a couple of salwar suits and one saree, a Kolkata cotton one . I loved cottons and Kolkata cotton was world-renowned. Sudhanshu picked a couple and Mom got 4 sarees. We hogged on the chat there and rasagullas. I got some packed for my colleagues at the radio station since we were leaving for Mumbai the next day. "Did you get some rasagullas for yourself? You love it," Mom reminded me and I got some packed for myself. She was happy here in Kolkata.

That evening, Sudhanshu took me to his house there and I met his father and relatives. I wore a cotton saree and was treated to Kolkata hospitality. His father was a theatre enthusiast and Sudhandhu updated him on his work and they said they came for the play on the first day itself. "You are as good as your mom now," his father Debashish told me. I was thrilled to bits. "So what next?" he asked me and Sudhanshu. "I got a movie offer, Dad," he said and told he was yet to write the script.

Debashish was happy to hear that. "Good, Show them how to act," he told me and I grinned.

"it's a different platform, I will have to learn it," I said Debashish brushed it away. "Mark my words, you both will ace it." I was happy with that.

"Deb da," I said. "When are you coming to Mumbai?"

"I plan a trip twice a year and this time it will be after 1 month. I think your movie stint would have started. I want to see the sets and the shooting," he told Sudhanshu. "I will arrange it, Dad," he said. We left after a scrumptious dinner.

Mom was waiting in the lobby to meet us and asked me if it was a pleasant experience.

I said, "Yes, Mom, Deb da was very nice and the hospitality was excellent."

"Good," she said and looked at Sudhanshu. They smiled at each other. "Did you eat?" he asked her and she said she had dinner and then kept vigil.

I said I going to catch some beauty sleep and retired to my room in the hotel. I shared the room with a friend. She was fast asleep, so no questions from her. I slept soundly and was woken up by my roommate for breakfast.

We were leaving after breakfast to Mumbai by a flight. I got ready quickly and went down with my baggage and saw that everybody had done the same. We came to Mumbai and left for our individual homes. I enjoyed the flight experience. I told Sudhanshu that I would take a cab. He disagreed. He got a cab for both of us and my house was the first stop and he got down to ferry my luggage to my apartment and then left for his home.

I tried on all the new dresses and recounted the reviews in their newspapers, which I brought back for my scrapbook. I will do it tomorrow, I thought and slept the rest of the day and night. We were scheduled to do the play for 1 week in Mumbai and there was a break after that.

I received a couple of offers with me in the lead and I discussed with Sudhanshu and accepted one. The rehearsals for that would start a week after this play ended. I told them about my movie commitment and they agreed to let me go if the script was ready before their play ended.

It was a different setup and I was looking forward to working in it. I got back to the RJ job and distributed the gifts and sweets that I had got in Delhi and Kolkata to my friends. After Sudhanshu's play ended, we had a wrap-up party and I went in the cotton saree I had picked up in Kolkata.

Mom had the same idea as well. It was time to part. I felt some misgivings about the parting and she felt the same. She took me aside and sat with me and said, "Tara, I beg you, please let me explain my side of the story to you. I want a relationship with you. I am so very proud of you and I will die with an ache in my heart if you rebuff me again. Please."

I nodded my head and said I was ready to hear it.

"Tomorrow at my place. You can bring Sudhanshu. I have no objections." I agreed and went back to my group.

Sonal left soon after. "You will come?" she asked me before she left.

"I will, Mom," I said and she said, "Come at 11 AM. I will be waiting."

Sudhanshu came to my side with a smile on his lips, "11 AM?"

"Yes. are you free? I am invited to my mom's apartment to hear her story."

"I am most certainly free," he said. "I will pick you up at 10.30 AM. Now, are you ready to leave? You have to get up early for your RJing." I agreed and we left and I went to my apartment and slept. There were no misgivings on my part about tomorrow. I thought the timing was right and my angst against her had disappeared because of the close proximity all these days and my success played a part as well. I wasn't insecure anymore.

I went to the radio station with a song in my heart and a smile on my lips. My 1 hour went very well and the producers were happy with me. I asked them if I could leave at 10.30 and they agreed. "As long as you keep your listeners happy. No need to stay unnecessarily." I thanked them and left and waited in the foyer and saw Sudhanshu arrive at 10.30 AM sharp. He said, "You look like a million bucks."

"Do you recognise the dress?' I asked him."

"Kolkota," he said. He most certainly did.

We started towards my mom's apartment. I asked him if he knew where she lived. He said, "Yes, I went there once."

"Okay," I said. We were at her residence sharp at 11 AM. I waited for Sudhanshu to guide me about where to go. It was on the first floor and the apartment was in an upper-middle-class locality. I loved the feel of it. We went to her door I could hear her asking Mihir, "Are you sure the time is right? They haven't come yet." I rang the bell. "There they are," he said and he opened the door. It was a tastefully decorated home and I loved it. It was warm and classy. I should do something like this to my house, I thought.

"It's a beautiful house," I declared and Mihir and Mom smiled.

"I will do something like this to my house," I said. "I will help," Mom said.

"What about you?" Mom asked Sudhanshu. "It's a barren house," he replied. "Compared to this."

I went around the house and saw that it was a 2 bedroom apartment and that it was decorated beautifully and both the rooms were occupied. I was surprised but didn't share it with Mom, who was showing the house to me. "Yes, we sleep apart," she said with a smile. "Come, dear, Let me take you through my journey." We decided to stay in the drawing-room and Mom made tea for everyone. Lunch was prepared and I remembered that she was a fab cook. She sat down opposite me and started.

Sonal's point of view

"I met your father Avinash at after-party after a successful show opening. He was a friend of a producer and we hit it off and he started coming to all of my shows and we fell in love and we got married after a whirlwind romance and with our parents' blessings. He was not from the theatre world and was something of a male chauvinist and I looked beyond that. I was around 25 years and not too good a character analyst. He made it clear that after marriage, I would quit theatre and I thought I will be able to make him change his mind and went along with his rules. I took a break from my career and spent my time making him happy. We were happy and I became pregnant with you and we were over the moon. I missed theatre but I brushed it aside and focussed on you when you were born."

"You were our point of focus and I thoroughly enjoyed spending time with you until you were 4 years old. Then came the economic downturn and pink slips for a whole host of people in the IT industry. He was one of them. We were in a fix as no one was hiring and he was rejected everywhere as the economy went from bad to worse and out of sheer helplessness at the situation, I volunteered to work and he could stay at home and look after you. He agreed and I got plays one after the other and money started trickling in and he started drinking. At home, outside and he started neglecting you. We put you in a good school and I gave him a little to take care of his expenses and saved the rest."

"I went from play to play and got recognition as a good actor and I was happy with my career, but the home was a different story altogether. I used to hide the bottles when he was away as I was worried he would abuse you after drinking. But that didn't deter him. He started going to bars to drink with his vagabond friends. He used to lock you in the room and leave. I came across this one day when I came early from my rehearsals and saw the locked room and opened it to see you in the corner with your favourite doll weeping. That night I would have taken you and left. I should have done that. But it was my house and I asked him to leave."

I was startled. "Your house, Mom?"

"Yes, dear," she said. "I took it and handled the loan payments. I got 2 movies back then and did them as well. Money was not a problem for me. I wanted to get rid of him. My parents had passed on by then and I had no support and he capitalised on that. He started abusing me physically after that and I slowed down my career to focus on you. But whenever we were in the same space, we ended up yelling abuses at each other and that impacted you in a bad way. I learnt from Sudhanshu that he hit you once. When was it, dear?" she asked me.

I said, "I was grown up by then, Mom. I was around 14 years old and I got up in the morning to find the bruise on my cheek. He brought your makeup and hid it. I did it till it went."

"I was happy when he was diagnosed with a brain tumour. I refused to part with money for his treatment. He went to a government hospital and his treatment went on off and on for 4 years before he passed on. But once he was diagnosed with the disease, he grew distant and kept to himself. Once he passed on, you turned on me and blamed me for his death and I could see our relationship turning from bad to worse, so I decided to move out and try to get to see what I could do about the situation. You were 20 years old then and you were attached to theatre. I thought I could get back in your good books soon."

"Then I met Mihir. We met for a few days and then Mihir asked me to move in with him as I had to leave the premises I had occupied on rent. I moved in and we fell in love soon after, But it's platonic. I will marry him after your approval, I thought and Mihir stood by my decisions with no complaints and I am deeply thankful to him."

We both had tears in our eyes by then and Sudhanshu offered Tara his handkerchief. Tara took it and sat quietly for some time.

Over to Tara

"Avinash told me during one of those times when we were alone that you were in and out of the beds of all the producers that approached you. He said he tolerated your presence in his house because of me. He told me one story or the other and blamed you for his illness. He said you spent more than you earned and his savings was the saving grace in the family. I believed him. I am sorry, Mom."

I leaned over to hug her and she cried more. "What about the 20 lakhs I got, Mom? Yours?"

"Yes, dear," she said.

"She started from scratch 4 years back," Mihir said. I was overwhelmed at the love Mom had for me. "Mom, you should take it back."

She said, "No, Tara. That's yours. We are doing a movie. There's good money there. I worked continuously for the past 4 years. I have a nest egg myself."

"Come," she said and took me to her room. The men also followed. She opened the wardrobe and there were gift-wrapped gifts there and she said she had bought dresses and jewellery for me and she gave them to me one by one. 2 jewellery sets and a whole lot of dresses. I was overwhelmed even more.

"Mom, what about your savings?"

"Oh, that will be more now with the movie and the plays. Plays have started paying more now and I am secured by Mihir as well. He is from the manufacturing industry and a big shot as well. If you say yes, I will marry him." They looked at me.

I said, "Yes, yes, yes. You must marry him."

They laughed and Mom and Mihir looked very happy. I wore the jewellery and they clicked pictures and there must have been at least 10 dresses and 5 sarees. The gorgeous saree in Delhi that she bought was for me. She took a suitcase and packed the gifts for me and the jewellery.

"I will not buy clothes for a while now," I said.

"Do you want to come and stay with me till you get married, Mom?" I asked her. She was excited at the idea. "Mihir, what do you say?"

"I will come along," he said. "I will sleep on the sofa."

Sudhanshu looked at me searchingly and asked, "What about me?"

"'My boyfriend," I said shyly and he grinned and nodded his head. "I will sleep on the floor." "Let's do it, "Sonal said. "But after lunch." Mihir and Mom packed. Then we had the most scrumptious lunch ever.

Mom had outdone herself. "I cannot live without any of this," Mihir declared. "The 2 of you have a week before another round of plays. Sudhanshu has work from home for a while. So let's make the most of it. I will take 2 weeks off. So let's hit the spots."

"Yes, Mihir," I said. Mom's tears were drying up and she looked happy, so did I.

"And the wedding…" I said.

"I will book a slot at the registrar's office and we will have a small party," he said. Mom agreed and we set out for my house.

Epilogue

Mom and Mihir got married.

Sudhanshu wrote another fab script for the movie and it was a success.

"I couldn't be happier," Tara said. "Not yet," said Sudhanshu. "There's more."

In Obesity and Health

I was in the mall with a friend who was trying on one dress after another and stood transfixed in the store. "Pari, why don't you look at the dresses?" Riya asked me. "Maybe they have some in your size." She burst out laughing. I looked at her icily and walked out and rode home on my scooty. I checked the tyres after the ride and made a mental note to have them checked in the petrol station. I yelled, "Mom, I am home." "Oh, so Dad doesn't deserve to know that," my dad teased me. I went and gave him a bear hug. He had gone to Bangalore on work from his office and was now back to Mysore 1 day early. He was an HR officer, having done his MBA in human resources.

I put the insult from my so-called friend in the back of my head in the morning and focussed on my dear parents. I was an only child and I had issues related to obesity. I am all of 25 years old and weigh 100 kgs with a height of 5'6". There is an extended family in Mysore from both my parents' sides of the family. But I keep to myself and my parents let me be. I was a star student and that was a feather in their caps as told by my parents to me.

My CA results were to be released in the afternoon and I was tensed, so I thought I would spend some time with some friends but that was a damp squib. I sat with my dad in the drawing-room and looked at the time. It was time but I made no move towards my laptop or to go to the institute. My dad picked up the laptop and typed in my number. The network was slow as it was all India portal and god knows how many had written the exam. Finally, it connected and I had passed with first-class marks. My father called the institute and asked if that meant I had secured a rank and they answered in the affirmative. That will be out in a couple of days, they said. I gave him a broad smile and went to hug my mother and to see what she was doing.

She was preparing my favourite sweets. She was that sure. "Well," she said. "If you passed, it will be a celebration and if you failed it, it will be to pick your spirits up. Is that explanation better?" she winked at me. "Dad?" I asked. "Why do you think he came home a day early, dumbo?" was the response. My dad was calling everyone he knew and telling them about my score. I was ecstatic with the result and about the happiness that gave my lovely family.

"So what will my princess like as a gift from her father?" he asked. I said, "Permission to apply for a job in Bangalore and if I get it, they should go with me. And it's not negotiable, Dad and Mom." He said, "Check and mate." He looked at my mom and raised his eyebrows. "What is your verdict, sweetheart?" he said. My mom said, "We go wherever she goes." So it was settled. "Next wish, my princess?" he asked. I said, 'That's all I will ever need, Dad."

We ate a hearty lunch and sat down to send job applications to top companies in Bangalore. We decided to wait for 2 days before sending them as I would get the rank from the CA institute by then.

I went up to my room to relax a bit as per my parents' orders. I sat by the window and thought about my life. It was perfect except for my obesity. I had hypothyroidism and that was the reason for my weight gain when I was a teenager. Though I knew about the causes and how important it was to maintain my weight. I would get serious issues due to my obesity, especially my heart. I couldn't bring myself to train in a gym under a tutor. My parents mentioned it once and I procrastinated. They left it at that. I went through college and life till now being made the butt of jokes from my so-called friends. There was not one friend in Mysore I will miss, I thought, so I was ready to start afresh in Bangalore. Maybe join a gym. I needed some motivation and I was sure it was in a multinational company in Bangalore.

My dad's office had their head office in Bangalore, so he could get a transfer there. They were asking him to move for the past year. It was a bigger opportunity there, but he was stalling it so that my studies were done and we can move lock, stock and barrel to the capital city of Karnataka. My mother wrote columns for a magazine and she can do it from anywhere. So the move did not displace anyone. A new beginning for everyone. My mom was 50 and goes by the name Namrata and my dad was 52 and is called Vishnu. They had a couple of close friends that were based out of Bangalore.

I got a call from the CA institute the next day. I stood second in the country and they said they would need a photo to put it in the newspaper. I said I would drop it in the office the next day. My mom picked a picture which she loved of me in a pink salwar suit and gave it to me. I grinned and said, "But the weight is still there," Mom. She said, "You look beautiful, Pari, just like your name."

I went to the office to drop off the photo and they gave me a letter which had all the details, my mark sheet would be sent home soon they said. I would also receive a completion certificate from the institute. If there was a change in address, we had to submit it in the office. I got the timelines and left. I smiled at a couple of known faces and that was about it.

I went home and gave copies of my credentials and sent the job applications with the rank letter and waited. I got a response from all 4 companies I had approached. They wanted to set up an interview. I responded by saying I would be available next week for the interview. My parents accompanied me to Bangalore and we rented rooms in a hotel and I went with my dad for the interviews. They said they would get back to me and we went around Bangalore and went back to Mysore after a couple of days.

I got a position in 3 out of 4 interviews I attended. I picked the company based on the discussion with my parents. I dropped an acceptance to the chosen company and we went around the shifting phase. My dad had also procured a position in Bangalore which was actually a promotion which he had kept a secret from us. He had the facility to work from home and I urged him to use it as he had not taken a break in his career. He agreed. We decided to board the Mysore house and take a flat in Bangalore and then maybe sell one of the sites my dad owned (He had 2 in Mysore) and buy a 3 bedroom flat in Bangalore. We decided to take it slow and not rush into anything.

The broker in Bangalore showed us 2 or 3 bedroom flats in the area near my office and we picked one. As it was a temporary arrangement, my mom was okay with it. My dad raised his brow and pretended to wipe the sweat from his brow at my mom and we laughed. "So soon, sweetheart," he said. My mom said, "Enjoy it while it lasts," and told the broker we would go with a furnished flat as that was the option offered by the owner.

We settled in and soon it was time for my first day at work. I picked the pink salwar suit that my mom liked so much and took my parents' blessings and left for work. As I thought about it, I felt a sense of achievement that I had reached this stage in my life. I took a deep breath and booked an auto in ola. My parents came down to see me off and I left home and entered into the world of adults.

I reached my office with some time to spare. I went to the reception and picked up my ID badge and wore it and went up to my assigned floor and stood there undecided when a hand tapped my shoulder and asked for an introduction. It was a very handsome man in his prime, say around 30 years of age and a ready smile. He knew he was irresistible, I concluded. I said, "Pari Vishnu," and he stuck out his hand and said, "Ritwick Iyer."

We shook hands and he said, "You are in my team." He said he was the functional manager and I was his reportee from today in business finance. I smiled and my dimples appeared in my cheeks and he said, "Charmed." I said, "Right." He smiled at the derision in my voice. "You are beautiful," he said and left.

"I will send you help," he said and his secretary came and helped me with my seat and gave me a list which had all the permissions that I had got for the apps, databases and websites which I would be using during the course of my work. I settled down and was checking the apps when I was surrounded by my team. I presumed this as Ritwick among them. There was a round of introductions and then they went to their seats. "Settle in and then we will start work. "

I said I was ready. "Then come this way with your laptop," he said and waited for me. I went with him to his cabin and we worked there till lunchtime. It was learning on the job and there was no specific training period allocated. I wanted it that way so I was happy. Ritwick said, "You have a sharp mind." I thanked him and went to my seat.

"If you don't have anyone to eat with, you are welcome to join me," he said and since I had spent the entire morning with him, I said I didn't know anyone else well enough to join them for lunch.

I went to wash my hands and I could overhear some women in the washroom whispering loudly. "He is being kind to her. He most definitely does not have a crush on her. She is huge." Then they laughed. "I heard that she was a wiz. Maybe that is it."

I smiled and left. Maybe that is it, I thought to myself and joined him. Lunch was good, appealing and tasty. He told me about his life. He lived with his mom as his parents were divorced and his father had a new family. They hardly met. "My mother is about 53 years old and very active," he said. "I'm lucky to have her as a mother," he said and looked at me expectantly.

"I live with my parents and am an only child as well," I said. "We shifted from Mysore to Bangalore for this job." Ritwick said he came from Mumbai to Bangalore for the job. "The company is very good and ranked in the top 3, but then you would know that," he said and I smiled. He gazed at me and then started eating. When we were done. He asked, "Friends?"

"I could use some good friends," I said.

"Me too. "

We went back to work and I was done by 6 and went to his cabin to clear it with him. It was a flexi hour job and had to be approved by the manager. "Wait for 10 minutes and I will drop you. This is a rush time and you won't get a cab or an auto." I had checked before I went to his cabin and knew that he was right. I agreed and went back to my bay area to my seat.

"Oh some people are soo lucky," those 2 women I overheard in the afternoon said. "We have been trying to catch his eye for 2 months and no luck so far. Look at you, you bagged him on the first day. What is the secret mantra?" they asked. I just looked at them with no expression

"Oh, we forgot to introduce ourselves. I am Preeti and this is Vanitha." I gave them a slight nod and waited for some more venom, but they left hurriedly. I looked beyond our group's bay and saw a man. He gave me a nod and left. Ritwick came out and we left for home. He had a luxurious car and it was a comfortable ride to my house. I explained my thoughts about getting my own house and he agreed. He said he would refer a broker if needed. I thanked him and invited him home. He came up with me. My dad was at home and so was my mom. I introduced him as my manager. He sat for a bit and had tea and then left saying his mother was alone. "She worries," he said. My mother said, "Bring her here, we need some friends. Our friends are mostly in Mysore." "Mostly, Mom?" I asked. "Yes," she said. My mom and dad's favourite friend had also shifted to Bangalore and they were happy about that.

Ritwick agreed readily. "When should I bring her? This Saturday?" I looked at him surprised. He said, "She needs something more in her life than just me." We agreed. So it was fixed for Saturday. He thanked my parents and left. "See you tomorrow. I will have to go this way to work. You can check the map," he said and told me he would pick me up at 9.30. I agreed and said I would meet him downstairs. I looked at my dad and he nodded. "So that's that. Good night, you lovely people," he said and left.

I asked my dad if he knew about the gym facilities in the society. He said, "Let's go and find out," and held out his hand. I grabbed it and held it and we went to the president of the association and asked if we had to submit special fees for monthly use of the gym. He said it was included in the maintenance bill and there was no extra payment. He said, "There will be a trainer from 7 AM to 7 PM. But the gym is open 24 hours a day."

We thanked him and went to check the place out. Since it was 10 minutes to 7, there was a trainer and I asked him if he would be willing to take on me as a trainee as I wanted to lose weight. He smiled and said, "I am up for the challenge if you are. Lots of hard work and perseverance."

I said I wanted to do it. "So come at 7 in the morning and we will work out for 1 hour every day." I said 7 to 8 suited me as I had to leave for work at 9.30 AM. He agreed and left. The gym was well equipped and I was raring to go. My dad looked at my enthusiasm and smiled. At last, he thought and looked at the door and saw my mother there. They smiled at each other. And I asked them, "Why don't you also work out?" They said it was a tempting thought and maybe for 30 minutes. "We will come tomorrow and check with the trainer." I was satisfied with the answer. We went back home.

The next morning I got ready for the gym and asked my parents how long did they think I would be able to wear western wear to the office. My mom said 6 months. "So soon, Mom," I asked. She handed me an article on weight reduction and I quickly scanned it and kept it in my room and left for the gym. The trainer was already present and he had arranged the equipment for me and he explained the routine to me and said the routine would change based on my improvement every week or maybe sooner.

I got down to work and my parents arrived and observed. They didn't want to disturb the trainer. Once he was sure I got the routine and was working as per his instructions, my dad approached him and said he wanted to do some cardio exercises and recommended exercises for my mom. The trainer was pleased. He said, "I wish more people thought of this as your family has done." He drew up routines for my parents for a half hour and helped them with it, always keeping an eye on me.

I was sweating buckets and my dad handed me a bottle of water and we both looked at the trainer and he nodded. That was allowed, and I gulped it down and started again thinking of all the pretty dresses I could wear. After I was done, he asked me to check my weight. The machine showed 99 kgs. I was pleasantly surprised. My trainer Madhu said the week's running around could be the reason for it. "We will check next week," he said. Weekly tests. I agreed and my parents thanked him and so did I and we went up to our routine. At 9.30, I went down and Ritwick arrived on time and we left for work.

Today, we worked as a team, as the consolidation of a report was needed and each team member had responsibility for their portion of work. I was the consolidation manager and other than me, there were 4 more in the team reporting to Ritwick. We sat in the conference room and prepared a report that was very good, I thought to myself. A lead from accounts came and said he had a complaint to be given to our manager because of the time we were spending in the conference room. I didn't say anything. The others from the team laughed and introduced me to him. "Pari meet Ravi." I said hello and he left. Ritwick came in a moment later and I said, "Rit, a petition is on its way."

He laughed and said, "Pun, I thought it was for fun."

"Intelligent man is an oxymoron," I said. "Moron, I thought it was more on," he said.

Ravi put his head inside and said, "It is in fact a truism."

"Oh, no, it's a euphemism," I said and there was applause all around.

"I will write this down," Ravi said and then glared at Ritwick and left. Ritwick laughed and said, "He wanted you in accounts. but I pitched in for business finance and we got you."

I was flattered. I made a mental note to thank Ravi later. "Thanks, Ritwick," I said and we got back down to work. He said it was best report he had seen in a while and we beamed.

"The layout is Pari's design, and we worked on our pieces. Let's keep this as a standard," he said and went to present it to his superiors. We went back to our desks and waited. He came back in an hour and beamed at us. "Team lunch tomorrow. Your choice. Company will pick up the tab." We were happy about a job well done. Ritwick said, "I am going to invite Ravi, and we burst out laughing." "Yo, Ritwick" Ravi yelled from across the hall. "I heard what happened upstairs. I will come to lunch. She will look for a change in 2 years as per company policy and I will be there for her and your team."

"My whole team?"

"Yes," he responded.

Ravi came across and congratulated Ritwick and said, "Deeply jealous," and left. We looked at Ritwick questioningly. "Everyone upstairs (superiors) appreciated the report. They wanted all the reports to be as comprehensive as ours was." We smiled and looked at each other.

"Can we do the same with all our reports to our superiors?" he asked and we nodded our heads vigorously.

"Okay, then let's do it tomorrow. I will book the conference room," he said.

As we left for home that day, Ritwick said he hoped his mother was able to make friends with my parents. "I hope she finds joy in her life," he said. When he was little, she used to sing bhajans and movie songs, but she stopped it abruptly and he had no idea why. I relayed the news to my parents that evening and they said they would try to make friends with Ritwick's mother, as according to him, she was lonely.

Soon Saturday approached and Ritwick brought his mother, Sharada to my house. She was a beautiful woman and she had worn a simple salwar kameez. We sat in the drawing-room for a little while and my mother asked that Ritwick and I go to my room or around the campus. I showed him my room and the house and then took him to the gym and proudly showed him the equipment and introduced him to my trainer. Ritwick asked, "Why are you training in the gym?"

"Rit, the answer is obvious," I said. "Look at me."

"Whatever you say," he said and looked. "Oh, but, not butt, your face... is the most beautiful face I have ever seen."

I was taken aback and said, "Thanks." My face turned crimson. He smiled and said. "Let's go up to your house. I want to see how my mom is doing."

We went up to my house and saw that his mother was having a good time with my parents. She looked at us and said, "About time Let's go home. I think they have had enough of us." "On the contrary…" my mom said and hugged her. "You will eat lunch with us and then we are going shopping, why don't you both join us?" Ritwick said, "We will, Aunty" and then looked at his mom. She smiled and agreed. Sharada showed them the stores she shopped in and it was a fun Saturday. They left in the evening and my parents told Sharada that they expected to meet often if that was okay with her. I would love to. "Next time, my house. I will cook lunch," and we agreed.

That evening my parents and my mom said Sharada had mentioned her singing to them. "She is a strong woman," said Vishnu. But she needs to lighten up and enjoy the journey and with a partner. I smiled, "I knew it. Who do you have in mind?"

"Damodar," Vishnu said and I clapped her hands. "My favourite among your friends, Dad. But we need Ritwick's permission."

"Bring him up when he drops you any day next week. I plan on working from home the whole of next week, Dad said and I agreed.

Work was excellent and I blossomed under Ritwick's guidance and my team was good. I made friends with all 4 and sometimes the entire team along with Ritwick went for lunch together and I settled in.

One day as I sat with my laptop getting a complicated report in place, I got a call from my mother. She said,

"Come straight to the hospital in the neighbourhood ASAP." I couldn't get any other information from her and rushed to Ritwick's cabin to get his permission. He said he would come along and when I told him that the report was almost done and I would finish it at night. He said that would be great and we went to the hospital and saw my mother weeping and sitting alone in the waiting room.

When she saw me she ran and hugged me. "Mama," I asked. "Who? Where is Dad?"

"He is inside, child," she said. "Vishnu suddenly collapsed and I called the ambulance and the doctors are checking," Said Namrata. Ritwick swore and went running to the nurse's station to ask for an update. Tears were flowing unabated from both our eyes. Namrata called Damodar, their friend and he said he would come in 10 minutes. Ritwick called his mother who had become a very good friend of my parents. She was shocked and said she will come in an auto as soon as she got one.

Ritwick knocked on the door where my dad was taken and entered. He remained inside for a good 10 minutes and then came to us and told us that it was a stroke and his left side was paralysed. Other than that he was okay. He told my mom, "You can visit him," gesturing to me to go with her. I nodded and we went to his bedside. My mom was partly relieved and partly crushed. "I thought we lost you," she said and hugged him.

"This is just a stroke, we will recover in no time," I said and both my parents smiled at me. Sharada and Damodar had arrived and were waiting outside. My dad, whose voice was slightly slurred, asked me to bring them in as well as Ritwick. He strictly told me, "Work should not suffer." I nodded wiping my eyes.

Ritwick was talking to the doctor and getting details about what we should be doing for his recovery. Physiotherapy, tablets, visits to the hospital, etc. I went and got introduced to the treating doctors. They said he should be in the hospital for a week and after that, he could be discharged. I thanked them profusely and asked about the possibility of a full recovery. They said 100%. That was such a relief, I almost laughed out aloud. "He will make it in record time," I said and they agreed. I told Ritwick, "Dad wants to see all his visitors." He smiled and walked with me to his room where Vishnu held court.

I volunteered to go home and bring my mom's clothes as she would be staying with my dad during the duration of his stay in the hospital. Namrata agreed and Ritwick stood up to give me the ride. Everyone else stayed put. My dad asked me to call his office and tell them what had happened. I nodded and we left.

Ritwick asked me during the drive to my house whether I would be okay staying by myself for a week at night. I gave him confirmation. We went home and packed my mom's stuff, called Vishnu's office and they gave an indefinite time off for my dad and said they would handle the insurance part of it. We went back to the hospital in an hour's time, and by then, our elders had done all the planning. Sharada would be staying with me in my house till dad was discharged and everyone would come to the hospital every day. Mom had got permission from the doctors. Ritwick looked at me and we smiled in relief.

Ritwick gave me a dongle to connect to the internet at the hospital the next day and said I could work from the hospital and my calls had been scheduled for 7 PM when I would be at home. I could go to the hospital at 10 AM and had to leave at 5 PM. I continued with my gym practice and had breakfast prepared by Sharada with some help from me. We both went to the hospital together.

Ritwick came in the afternoon for an hour and went back to work. Damodar also came at the said timings. My dad was responding to the treatment very well and the doctors were happy. "I have a lot of work to do still. I'm not ready to go yet," Vishnu said. I hugged him with tears in my eyes and said, "Promise, Dad."

"I promise, my child," he said. The doctors were trying to convince my mom to appoint a male nurse at home for one month as it would ease her burden a little. Sharada asked me to talk to my mother and I said, 'Mom, let's do it." Namrata said only for one month and agreed.

On the said date, Ritwick came in his car and we bundled into it. My dad and my mom came in the ambulance. I had done some decorating in the house and everyone was pleased as my father laughed out in delight. "Did you paint, my dear?" he asked and I said, "Yes."

I still teared up every time he addressed me. It was touch and go. I made a mental note to take him to the gym regularly as he was not regular previously. He would have some calls in the morning. All that should change, I thought.

I worked from home for a week and then started going to office as dictated by my dad. He was responding well to the therapy and the therapist gave him 2 months of intensive training. We agreed and that set a routine for the coming days. My dad recovered bit by bit and my office provided all the facilities and helped me out during this time. I was extremely grateful to Ritwick as he had set the ball rolling.

After 1 month, my dad was able to sit in a wheelchair with some help and some sensation had returned in his left side. We decided to keep the same team, so the male nurses' tenure was extended for 1 more month. Sharada and Damodar came almost every day and they became part of the family. Same with Ritwick. I started noticing Sharada was getting closer to Damodar and they became thick friends. I mentioned it to my parents and they agreed. Everyone had noticed it except Ritwick. Vishnu said he would talk to Ritwick himself. The slurring of his speech was slowly disappearing.

In the middle of all this, Ritwick got instructions that he had to be present for a conference in Tokyo and some work with the team there. We were all happy except him.

He told my dad, "Mom has to stay alone." My dad said, "No, she won't. She can come and stay with us and it's only for a week."

Sharada was okay with the plan as well as Ritwick. I shopped with him as per our parent's instructions. He needed to get warm clothing, so we went in search of it and got some very good stuff for him.

My dad asked to speak to me and him and we obliged. He told him about the closeness his mother and Damodar had achieved and said he would soon be talking to them about getting married. "Not sure if you noticed my lad," my dad said.

Ritwick was in shock and felt deeply ashamed that he had not noticed it. He asked if he should do something. My dad said he would handle it. Damodar was in his team in the same company and he earned well. He just never got married when everyone else was. "A very good soul…" my dad told him and he said he would make a good husband to Sharada. Ritwick slowly came out of his shock and touched my dad's feet and said, "Thank you, Uncle. I need you, please recover soon," and my dad said, "Likewise, my dear lad."

We went out and mom went in to give my dad company. Ritwick noticed the closeness his mother shared with Damodar and went near to hear what he was telling my mom. He was encouraging her to revive her singing. He said he will arrange for whatever she needed. A teacher or books or musical instruments. "I will learn whatever you want me to learn and we can make an orchestra."

I noticed Ritwick getting all possessive about his mom and he went and sat next to Damodar. Sharada noticed it. She asked me, "What's with him?" Him being her son. "Aunty, you know how men are," I said. "Except for my dad." "Oh no," Sharada said. "Ask your mom, dear. They are all the same." We both laughed.

Ritwick noticed our closeness when I got up to hug his mom. He took a deep breath and asked me, "You have lost weight. How much?" "She is now 90 kgs. She lost 9kgs in one month. Isn't that fantastic?" Sharada interjected.

To this, Ritwick smiled and congratulated me. "As long as it doesn't do anything to her face," he murmured, We all heard it and Sharada and Damodar smiled at each other. "Have you packed, son?" Sharada asked and Ritwick said, "Not yet, Mom. Will do it tonight." He was leaving early morning tomorrow. "Do you like it here?" he asked his mom.

"Absolutely, I love it. Lovely people and beautiful to the boot," she said and he looked sharply at me. I shook my head. Coincidence, we both thought.

Ritwick left with his mother soon after in the same strange mood. His mom was mightily amused, so were all of us except Damodar. "I need a word with Vishnu," he said and went to his room. I sat with my laptop and sent the explanation files I had prepared for Ritwick. He sent a relieved smiley. "Log in during my time, please," he said. 3 and a half hours ahead of India. I agreed. I sent a bon voyage message and logged off.

I shifted my gym sessions to the evening at 5 PM. It would be 8.30 PM in Tokyo and he would be having dinner, I thought. I told my parents that for a week, I would have to log in at 6 AM. They said, "Work is worship. Do it."

The next day Sharada came at 9 AM with her bag and we welcomed her. Damodar came at 10 AM. We got a message from Ritwick that he had reached safely and was headed for a conference. I went to my room and logged on. Soon, he was on the phone with questions, and I brought his attention to the files that I had sent him the previous night. Soon, he was equipped with the answers and he switched off his phone with strict instructions that I should not do the same. I had tea that was brought to my room by Sharada. "Oh, Aunty, I would have come to the kitchen. Please don't bother. "No bother," she said. "My son has become a bear with a sore head. So something from my side." We both laughed.

He showed extra concern to his mom. With messages telling her about what was going on bit by bit. Namrata and Sharada were sharing this with the men and they had a hearty laugh. So Vishnu asked Damodar first. "What are your intentions towards Sharada"

He said, "Marry her and take her to my house if she agrees."

Sharada said 'I love you' to Damodar. "Let's see what my dear son says." And they had a laugh as Ritwick was asking her if she had eaten and if she had, what did she eat.

Day 1 passed on well enough with Ritwick being on top of his presentations and he received accolades for the same from the superiors present there. He was happy.

I sent him a congrats smiley and he said, "Not without you." I sent a thanks and asked him if I could log off. I had a gym appointment. He said there was no need to beat my weight black and blue and throw it off. Some people look very attractive with some weight. I said, "I am targeting 80 kgs right now. I will take a call at the end of the month when I achieve it."

"Is that healthy?" he asked.

"10kgs every month. I am training under a qualified trainer," I said.

"Who knows what the truth is," he grumbled. "Tomorrow we will have a video call," he said and logged off.

The next morning he was in high spirits. No presentation that day, only listening he messaged

to both me and Sharada. He messaged before he logged off at 4 PM and asked me what to get his mother from Tokyo. I said some winter clothing. "I heard that they have the best clothing there," I said. "From?" he asked. "Damodar Uncle had visited Tokyo 2 years back and he told me," I said. He was speechless. "Okay," he said and logged off. Namrata was in my room and I showed her the messages. "These are priceless. Save them."

"Okay, Mom," I said and smiled.

The rest of the week passed by quickly with me on stand by and he was a star in Tokyo among the meet. I was happy. He was ecstatic. It was a video call in the evening before he logged off. He looked at me keenly and I was amused like his mother had been.

Ritwick came back straight from the airport to my house bearing gifts. He got me a jacket which was beautiful. And the size was at least 1 size small. He raised his eyebrows at me. "After 80 kgs, you should stop. Please!" he said and the elders were smiling.

"I will think about it," I said and saw that he had got lovely gifts and Japanese fans as well. My mom got 2 big ones. She said, "I will keep this inside. I will decorate our new house with these, Ritwick. Thank you."

My dad got a digital camera. He was enthralled with it. "Ritwick, you should help me with the instructions." Ritwick was mighty pleased. His mother got a kimono dress. "You can wear it at your wedding mom after the ceremony. For the party." Sharada teared up.

"So you approve?" she asked. Ritwick hugged her and wiped her tears and said, "What's not to like? Damodar uncle spoke to me before I left. I am happy for you and myself. I will miss you, Mom," he said.

"You should come with us to our house," Sharada said.

"Let's see how things pan out," he said, smiled and handed Damodar his gift. It was a watch.

"What did you buy for yourself, Rit," I asked. He showed me a jacket similar to mine. "The correct size," he said. He told me he had brought some trinkets for the team as well and some more fans. I thought he had done a fantastic job with the gifts and told him so. He beamed. He asked his mom, "For now, let's go back to our house. I would like to spend as much time as possible with you. I have to go to the office for an hour to appraise them with the situation and then need to chat with you." Sharada agreed and bid adieu for a short time.

They left and I prepared to leave for my gym practice. Vishnu asked Damodar what kind of marriage they had planned.

"The registar office and a small party for our friends, and if she wants to invite relatives, then them as well."

I had a song in my heart. "It felt so good to see Ritwick," I told them. "Mom, what about you?" I asked. She said, "Of course. You will be late if you don't go now."

I rushed out and went to the gym. I needed to get into that jacket. I worked extra hard that day and asked to see the weight. He allowed it. I was 85 kgs. "5 more," I muttered.

"Are going to stop at 80 kgs?" my trainer asked.

"For now, yes."

He said, "If you want, we can go down to 70 kgs. Think about it."

I said no, "80 kgs and not a kg more, not a kg less."

He laughed at that. "Whose book was it ?" he asked.

"Jefferey Archer."

"Not a penny more, not a penny less," Ritwick said from the doorway.

"You didn't leave?" I asked.

"I did but we decided to come back and discuss the marriage plans and fix the date. Purohit has come and they have given the day. It is 7th of next month. They are talking about who to invite. I thought I will come and check on you. Are you done?" he asked me.

I said, "Yes," wiping the sweat from my face with a hand towel.

"She wants to stop at 80 kgs. Can you influence her to go till 70 kgs," my trainer asked him. "Nope. I am in agreement," he said and we left as my mom had sent me a message: Stop flirting with Ritwick and join us. I was appalled. "Let's go," I said and we left the gym with a quick bye to my trainer.

The next day I left for office at the normal time. Ritwick dropped his mother and picked me up. The preparations for the wedding were going on. My dad was recovering in record time. The sensations on the left side had returned and he walked around with a walker. The male nurse was worth his weight in gold. He took my dad to the park downstairs and practised walking. My mom always accompanied them as did Sharada and I sometimes. Now that Ritwick was back, he also went along if the walk was assigned at the time when he was around.

We reached the office and I walked up to our floor. Ritwick joined me and we went to our bay/cabin. I had a letter on my desk. The director wanted to meet me. As I left my bay, Ritwick also emerged with the same message in his hand. We went up together and were asked to enter the conference room and we obliged. There was all the top management in the room and we were motioned to sit. "How is your father doing, Pari?" one of the directors asked me after introducing himself. "He is improving very well. He will be able to walk by himself soon. We are keeping our fingers crossed."

"And your mom, Ritwick? You refused to travel in the past because you didn't want to leave her alone."

"She stayed with Pari's family in their house," Ritwick disclosed. "We are family friends." "Close friends," he said.

One of them said, "We are promoting you, Ritwick and your team as well. You will be the CFO of your cluster and the finance controller will be Pari. We saw those explanation files my dear, it was pretty awesome. Your team will go with you as you have trained them. You choose who will fit where," they told Ritwick. Congratulations. Your name was reverberating in the conference halls."

"All credit to my team," Ritwick said. And we shook hands with them and left.

Our promotions came in the management bulletin and everyone knew about it. When I was walking across the bay, Ravi switched on the light and said, "And then God said…"

"Let there be light," I said and we laughed. He congratulated me. "I cannot touch the finance controller," he said. So better luck in next life and left. I went back towards my bay. "And what did he want?" asked Ritwick with a scowl.

"If you go to accounts, they will not have a position for you. It will be a demotion." I put up my hands and said, "Stop, Rit. It was just a congratulation and he told me about the unavailability of roles for me there." Ritwick's face cleared. "Okay then."

"He got it finally". "I have decided who gets what portfolio in our team. Let's have a team meeting. My assistant will send you an invite."

I said I would join.

I received the appreciation and promotion letters and gasped at my salary hike. I ran to his cabin and said, "Rit, do you think they made a mistake with my salary?"

He smiled and asked for the letter. He looked at it and said, "No. This is the number for a finance controller."

"You gave gifts to everyone. Now it's my turn," I said. "Then let's go shopping," he said. "Yes. I will inform Mom we will be slightly late."

I bought ethnic clothes for everyone including Ritwick. I asked him to wear the designer wear I had picked for him. He obliged and looked like a successful man in his prime. I winked at him and said, "You look like a model, Rit."

"Likewise, sweetheart."

"Only you don't seem to agree."

"80 kgs, stop gymming and focus on me." His eyes were intense and I could see a slight twinkle. I said, "Okay, Rit, whatever you say."

"Does that mean you are okay to go on dates with me?"

I said yes and looked at him shyly. "How long for this milestone?" he asked.

"1 more week," I said and he said he could wait.

We went home bearing gifts and everyone were extremely happy. I went and sat near my dad and said, "Happy, Dad?" He said, "Ecstatic," and stood up and took 2 steps and then Mom came and held his hand and took him to the sofa. "Come here, child," he said.

"Happy?" he asked me. I teared up again. "Yes, Dad."

"This is one of the best days in my life," Ritwick said and asked for updates in the marriage preparations.

"I am going to wear this saree for the wedding and the kimono for the party," said Sharada.

Ritwick said, "We need to tell the elders something."

They looked at us. Both our moms held hands and looked at us. Ritwick said, "We have developed feelings for each other and we want to further take it by going on dates. We need all of your permission."

They all grinned and they said we can most definitely go on dates. There was no objection from their side. We thanked them and I ran to my room, he burst out laughing.

We went on dates once a week and our feelings developed into something stronger and it was love. We decided we would tell everyone after Sharada and Damodar's wedding. Not that they needed telling. All they had to do was look at us together and they would get it as our team in the office had done. They congratulated us and we shook hands. Ritwick was happy to let people know I realised. I was still shy about it. He said he would handle it. But some teasing was inevitable, especially from Ravi.

"Just imagine Rit the wick if she had come to my team."

"I would have wooed her across the floor," said Ritwick. "Both for work and for me. For she enhances me and upgrades me and soon with marriage, she will enslave me."

I blushed and everyone clapped.

At home, we were busy with the guest list and location fixing and the food menu. Sharada wanted some key rituals to be performed and she said it would be graced by Vishnu and Namrata. The number of people came to around 30, so they decided to take on have the registrar come to the location and finish the registration on the same day. The party in the evening was scheduled in a 5-star hotel and was funded by Ritwick. There was only a week to go.

At the gym, I achieved my target and asked my trainer to tell me how to maintain this weight. He said some amount of training was still necessary and I needed to maintain the nutrition chart which he had given me when I joined. I took a selfie with him and gave him an idol of Ganesha as a thank you gift. He was happy but still stuck on the 70 kgs.

"Let me know if you change your mind."

I said, "Most definitely."

The D day arrived for Sharada and Damodar and we went to the Chowltry. Ritwick had come with his mother and Damodar with us. I was dressed in a Mysore silk saree and minimum jewellery. My hair was in a plait. Ritwick was dumbstruck.

"Vishnu Uncle, can I take a photo of us together?" he yelled. My dad gave a thumbs up and we took a selfie. He was dressed in the dress which I had gifted and looked pretty awesome.

The wedding went as per plan and our guests were polite and happy for the two of them. The food was excellent. We told them to please grace the evening party.

For the evening I had a pink gown which my mom helped select for me and I wore the jacket on top of the dress. "You look yummy."

My mom hugged me and so did my dad. He was now near normal. After a 2 week rest, he planned to join his office again. They had sent their approval. Sharada looked like a million bucks in the kimono. The party was a success and the newlyweds went to Ritwick's house. He was pleasantly surprised.

"But I thought you will go to Damodar's house, Mom," he said.

"Not until you are married," said his mom. "You are our priority." He was happy and agreed vigorously.

The next day at work an apparition came visiting. Her name was Mona and she was Ritwick's ex. One of the two relationships he had before me. The first one had married as per her status and this was the second one.

"Ravi called me to join back and I thought why not?" she told me. "I was his blue-eyed girl," she said with a tinkling laugh.

Her makeup was loud and she wore a mini skirt with high heels.

"Ravi sits over there." I showed her the bay from my seat.

"Of course," she said. "I know all about that," and she went to his bay. Ravi downright denied calling her and showed her the door. "She was a liability, why would I call her?" he told Ritwick and me

When she saw Ritwick, she jogged to him and hugged him. He warded her off and came and stood with me.

"Oh does that mean you have gotten over me, my beloved?" she screamed.

I held back my laughter and let a smile come over my face. Ritwick saw it and looked relieved.

"Thanks," he said and I grinned at him. "Sharada had rejected her. What did you see in her?" I asked.

"She was good at her work and I thought that must mean something. But later Ravi told me that she used to get her work done by others and claimed credit. When Ravi got to know, he told me immediately and I cut all relations with her."

"Ritwick, darling, I am still pining for you," she yelled.

Ritwick was getting angry by the minute. They took her outside and told her never to come back again.

"I know his house," she yelled again. I was concerned at that comment.

Ritwick said, "If that happens, we will approach the police. Tonight we will all sleep in your place."

"Agreed," I said.

"Ask Dad, love."

I told him. He agreed. We left soon after and we didn't encounter her on the way. Ritwick got my dad and Damodar together and explained the situation in the office. Namrata and Sharada came and sat down. Dad told Ritwick, "Let's go to the nearest police station and file a complaint just in case. We should all stick together till this blows over."

We all agreed. Ritwick and Damodar left and came back in an hour's time. There was a constable posted at our door.

Dad called the association president and told him about what happened and he got permission for the constable. At about 10 PM, we heard a rock hit one of our windows. Ritwick and Damodar rushed down and we went to the window. The constable said, "Stay away from the windows," and went down. There were some 4 miscreants present there and they had stones in their hands. Dad had called the police station and a police jeep arrived and bundled them into the jeep along with Mona, who was hiding behind a parked car.

Ritwick got his car around and his mom and Damodar left with him in his car. We went back to the house and I closed all windows as per Vishnu's orders. We waited for about 30 minutes and they appeared.

By then Namrata had made some bhel puri. They said if we press charges, then they would file the FIR. Or else they would be given a warning. Damodar wanted to get Vishnu's advice on this.

"Anyway, we will not let them go for 2 days," the inspector said. Vishnu asked about their previous history and it was clean. He wanted to talk to them and then let them go if he was convinced. Ritwick said, "Then we will go there tomorrow morning. All of you sleep tight."

We retired to our rooms and Mom prepared the drawing-room couch for Ritwick.

The next day after breakfast the men left for the police station and we sat in the drawing-room and planned a lunch spread with responsibilities for all 3.

"Now you have to learn to cook, Pari," my mom said and I smiled and nodded my head. They both looked at me and then went to hug each other and then came to me for a hug.

"We wanted to tell you all after your wedding, Aunty," I said.

"It's mom now," she said. They added sweet to the lunch spread.

It was about 2 and a half hours before they came back and they had decided to let them go, but the police would dig for information for 1 week and then let them go, they said.

"We have some good news for you, Ritwick," his mom said. He looked at her.

"Damodar and I had decided last night that if you want to marry Mona, we are okay with it."

The men looked aghast at her. Ritwick went and hugged her. "Thank you, Mom. The name is Pari," he said.

"I wanted to ask her dad's permission."

"Now," Dad said on the couch.

We could hear the good-hearted ribbing between the 3 of them. He finally got permission.

Epilogue

Mona and her gang never intruded on Pari and Ritwick.

The families were in and out of each other's houses.

They bought flats in the same address and next to each other.